A SU

'Do you love him enough to make that kind of sacrifice?'

Nurse Dee Latimer had finally decided that her relationship with Bobby Carr was not going to work; her job was too demanding and his dangerous career was too worrying for her to live with. Then Bobby was seriously injured—and Dee knew that she could not abandon him now. But surgeon Greig Meredith thought otherwise . . .

Sarah Franklin lives in Cambridgeshire with her husband, cat and a 'very bossy but lovable' dog. She has always been interested in anything medical. Both her daughters, before marriage, were working in the field of medicine; one as a nurse, the other as an aesthetician, and Sarah herself has been a keen member of the St John Ambulance Brigade and holds their certificates for nursing and first aid. Writing and researching the medical content of her books takes up most of her time, but her hobbies include gardening, the theatre and music as well as 'dabbling with a paint brush'. This is her fifteenth Doctor Nurse Romance. Other titles include *The Doctor from Wales*, *The Kiss of Life* and *No Ordinary Nurse*.

A SURGEON'S SACRIFICE

BY

SARAH FRANKLIN

MILLS & BOON LIMITED
ETON HOUSE   18–24 PARADISE ROAD
RICHMOND   SURREY TW9 ISR

First published in Great Britain 1987 by Mills & Boon Limited

© Sarah Franklin 1987

Australian copyright 1987 Philippine copyright 1987

ISBN 0 263 75804 4

Set in 10 on 11 pt Linotron Times
03–0887–57,200

Photoset by Rowland Phototypesetting Limited Bury St Edmunds, Suffolk Made and printed in Great Britain by William Collins Sons & Co Ltd, Glasgow

CHAPTER ONE

DEE LATIMER glanced at her reflection in the mirror over the scrub-room sink as she scrubbed up for the emergency appendicectomy. With her red-gold hair firmly tucked out of sight under the blue theatre cap her oval face looked fragile and vulnerable; even she could see the lines of strain and tiredness around her eyes. They had been especially busy today. Theatre One was the emergency theatre and though the work was varied and interesting it was hardly ever possible to rely on getting away on time.

Through the mirror she could see the clock on the opposite wall. Ten past three—and they were preparing for an urgent appendicectomy. Ward E2, which was the emergency 'on take' ward, had alerted them ten minutes ago to say that a patient had just been admitted and was on the way up. Dee sighed as she elbowed the tap lever to the off position and turned towards the nurse waiting to help her on with a fresh pair of sterile gloves. Bobby would be well into his practice session by now. He would have given her up. He was as unused to her unsocial hours as she was to the hair-raising risks he took as a motorcycle racer. But she had *promised* this time— promised to be there timing each lap with the stop-watch as he tried out the new bike after its rebuild; lending her encouragement and moral support, much as she hated his racing. After the row they'd had—after the compromise Bobby had finally agreed to, she had felt it specially important that she should show how willing she was to keep her part of the bargain. If *only* the shift could have finished on time for once . . .

'Are you feeling all right, Nurse Latimer?' Mary Fairchild, the Theatre Sister, was looking at her anxiously. 'You're looking a bit peaky. I know it's been a long session, and if . . .'

'No! I'm perfectly all right, thank you, Sister.' Dee pulled herself together sharply. She was acutely aware that her job of scrub-nurse held great responsibility and she was proud of the status she held, having worked hard to attain her theatre certificate. It was quite unforgivable to allow one's thoughts to wander—for personal problems to encroach. In the theatre there is room for nothing in the mind but the job in hand, she admonished herself silently. She smiled reassuringly at Sister Fairchild before her mouth was covered by the fresh mask Nurse Hastings was waiting to tie for her. Hopefully she put all her confidence and efficiency into her eyes as she said: 'With a bit of luck this will be the last for this shift.'

Bobby Carr pulled the crash helmet on firmly over his unruly fair hair. After fastening it securely under his chin he glanced at his watch. Obviously she wasn't coming now. Better give her the benefit of the doubt. It must be that damned job of hers; it was always holding her up—gumming up the works and causing trouble between them. But he couldn't say much; he wasn't exactly noted for reliability himself! He grinned to himself. Come to that, if it hadn't been for Dee's job they would never have met in the first place. He'd been a patient in her ward eighteen months ago when he'd crashed and gone into hospital with a broken leg. Dee had only just passed her finals at the time, the archetypal bossy staff nurse—trying her hardest to remain po-faced. She wouldn't laugh at his jokes—was forever ticking him off for disrupting the ward; doing her best to look as stern and frosty-faced as Sister. What a hope she'd had, with looks like hers! He grinned as he remembered the furious way her gorgeous green eyes had blazed when he'd grabbed her and kissed her as she was helping him out of bed one morning. She was the first girl he had actually had to pursue, and he had found it refreshing. She wouldn't go out with him until weeks after he had been discharged from the hospital. A real challenge she'd turned out to be. But Bobby thrived on challenges, and he had won her over in the end—or had he? He frowned. Dee had done her share of winning too, much to his chagrin. He still couldn't quite believe that she had extracted that promise from him last night. He must have been mad! Give up racing after he'd won the Grand Prix, so that they could get married! The Grand Prix was only the beginning! Dee knew it as well as he did. He chewed his lip. He would have to think of some new way to win her round again. It'll be all right, he told himself with characteristic confidence as his face relaxed into a grin again. He couldn't remember a time when he hadn't been able to talk her round with kisses and sweet words. She was a strong-minded girl, but she would be the first to admit that she had a weakness where he was concerned.

He stood for a moment, his vivid blue eyes thoughtful as he surveyed the scene around him. Today it was fairly quiet, but this time next week the competitors would be arriving, setting up their mobile homes in the paddock, settling in their wives, girl-friends and back-up crews. Although the race wasn't for another ten days he could already feel the tension beginning to build, the air vibrated with the sound of engines revving at full throttle as other racers lapped the course, testing and practising. The place was alive with the familiar smells. Bobby breathed them in, savouring them; to him they were the sweetest scents in the world—the very essence of life and all that excited him; a mixture of dust and oil,

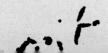

leather, petrol and hot metal. It filled his nostrils and scorched the back of his throat. He felt *good* in spite of Dee's absence, and he smiled across at his mechanic, waiting with the gleaming monster at the ready—the newly modified 500cc V4 that had been such a headache ever since it had arrived from the factory a week ago. Well, better get on and test her. This was the moment of truth. 'Okay then, Jim?'

Jim nodded. 'I think you'll find she rides easier now, Bob,' he said confidently. 'Not so twitchy. Try a couple of laps. Take it easy and see what you think.' He looked round. 'Dee not timing you today?'

Bobby shook his head as he sat astride the bike. 'She should have been. Something cropped up at the hospital, I guess. Bloody inconsiderate of people—needing operations on trial days, eh?'

Jim watched him as he revved the bike experimentally and rode off on to the circuit, accelerating briskly. The mechanic shook his head. He knew Dee Latimer would have been here if she could, even though it was obvious that she hated the track and all it stood for. He had watched the stormy affair from the beginning; watched with a fatherly concern. Those two young people would destroy each other if they weren't careful, he told himself sadly. They were totally unsuited—she with her caring concern for people and her dedication to her job; Bobby with his fatalistic attitude, his cavalier disregard for safety, especially his own. Dee wasn't like the girls who hung around the circuits ogling the racers, waiting to be picked up. She was steady, with feelings that went deep. That was the cause of half the trouble between them. She was the kind of girl who made commitments and stuck to them. Bobby would break her heart if she wasn't careful. He'd never give up racing—not for anyone; God only knew his parents had tried hard enough to get him to drop it. He loved it and all that went

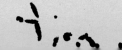

with it—the hordes of admiring girls; the adulation and excitement of winning; the highs and the lows. Jim of all people knew Bobby Carr well enough to know that he couldn't live without these things.

Douglas Thurman, the general surgeon, nodded to his houseman. 'Fine, you can suture now. Caught that one just in time. Another hour and we'd have had a perforation on our hands.' He turned away, removing his surgical gloves and dropping them into the bowl Sister Fairchild held for him. He smiled at her disarmingly as he pulled down his mask. 'I'll write it up before I go, but I'd appreciate a cup of tea and a sandwich—supposed to be playing golf with my bank manager at half four and I had to skip lunch. Lay it on for me, like a good girl, will you, Sister?'

By the time Sister Fairchild reappeared the patient had been wheeled away to the recovery room and Dee had already started counting the instruments on the trolley, checking them off against the list before the waiting auxiliary wheeled them off to the sluice. 'Honestly, I'm sure that man thinks I've nothing better to do than wait on him!' she said in an outraged tone.

Dee looked up. 'You know you love dancing attendance on him. Why pretend?'

Sister Fairchild's colour deepened. 'Well, he doesn't take proper care of himself now that he's a widower, and someone has to see that he eats. I draw the line at bringing it into the theatre, though. Sometimes I think he sees me as a sort of nanny!'

Dee was grateful for the mask that hid her smile. Everyone knew that Mary Fairchild had been in love with Mr Thurman for years. Why she bothered to pretend her interest was purely for his welfare no one knew. It was equally obvious that Douglas Thurman took

advantage of her quite outrageously, though Dee privately thought that he was so dedicated to his work that he'd need to be hit over the head with a statue of Eros before he'd succumb to love. She ticked off the last instrument on her list and pulled off her mask. 'You shouldn't let him take you for granted so,' she said. 'It isn't a good idea, always being there when you're needed.' She followed Sister into the sluice, pulling off her gloves and dropping them into the waste bin as she went. 'Tell you what, let *me* take him his tea and sandwiches. That'll give him something to think about!'

'Want to bet?' Mary Fairchild challenged. She looked at her scrub-nurse thoughtfully. 'You wanted to get away on time this afternoon, didn't you? Something important?'

Dee paused in the act of untying her theatre gown. 'I did rather, yes.'

When she didn't explain further Mary prompted her: 'That young man of yours?'

'It's the try-out for the Grand Prix,' Dee told her briefly. 'He has a new bike. It's been modified and he's been worrying over it. I said I'd go to the circuit to time him this afternoon. I'll be on duty on the day, you see, so I won't get to the race itself.'

Mary sighed. 'All that noise, and the terrifying speed! I can't think what anyone sees in it—to say nothing of the danger. Don't you worry?'

Dee sighed resignedly. 'I try not to. Bobby never seems to think of that side of it, though. But there are irritating disadvantages to my job too. We both have to try to be tolerant.'

In the nurses' changing room she showered and dressed in the clothes she had meant to wear to the circuit—well cut navy trousers and a crisp white shirt. Bobby liked her to look well groomed; he hated girls in scruffy jeans and tee-shirts. Dee put on a little make-up and brushed out the bright, collar-length hair. Might as well put in an appearance, even though it was too late. She remembered her promise to Sister just as she was picking up her bag. Mr Thurman's tray had just come up from the kitchen and was waiting on the table—ham and tomato sandwiches and a pot of tea. She picked it up and went along the corridor to the little office where the surgeons wrote up their reports. Knocking on the door, she heard the surgeon's gruff bark of: 'Come!' and, balancing the tray on one hip, she opened the door and walked in.

He sprawled untidily in the chair, his long legs splayed. He still wore his theatre greens. The cap, which he had obviously forgotten, had worked its way on to the top of his bushy grey hair and sat perched there, making him look for all the world like an oversized garden gnome.

'I've brought your tea and sandwiches, sir. Oh . . .' It was only then that she noticed that he wasn't alone. His visitor sat on the chair behind the door, a man with powerful broad shoulders and dishevelled thick brown hair that looked as though it needed cutting. The eyes that swept audaciously over Dee from top to toe and back again were a compelling hazel brown. He wore a well-worn brown leather blouson and jeans. She hadn't seen him before, but from his appearance she guessed that he was something to do with hospital maintenance —an electrician perhaps; she had heard that there was a vacancy in that department.

She put the tray down on the desk. 'I'm sorry, Mr Thurman, I didn't realise you had a visitor.'

The surgeon gave her his beguiling smile. 'This is Mr Meredith.' He pronounced it: Mer-*e*-dith. 'Perhaps you could bring him another cup? I'm sure he could drink a cup of tea.'

Dee felt put out. Why should she run about getting

cups for maintenance staff after working a long and arduous shift? At this rate she wouldn't get to the circuit before they packed up and went home! She was beginning to regret offering to bring Mr Thurman his tea. It was a waste of time anyway. Sister had won her bet—he hadn't even asked about her.

'Please don't bother for me. Time I was going anyway.' The stranger got to his feet and Dee saw that he was taller than she had first thought, almost six feet. His voice surprised her too—deep and rich, with more than a hint of a Welsh accent.

She turned to face him, colouring a little as she realised that her resentment must have been noticeable. 'Oh—are you sure? Only—only I *do* happen to have an appointment.' Her eyes were irresistibly drawn to the clock on the wall behind him, and he was quick to notice.

Mr Thurman broke in: 'Well now, I'm sure Mr Meredith would be happy to give you a lift, as he has to go too. Got to be off myself as soon as I've had my tea. I'll see you around, then, Meredith. Good afternoon.' He rose and ushered them to the door, closing it firmly behind them. It was typical of him. One minute he could be chatting away, the next minute he was dismissing you in mid-sentence.

Dee and the stranger found themselves outside the door without quite knowing how they got there. They smiled at each other hesitantly. Mr Meredith zipped up his blouson and raised an enquiring eyebrow.

'Well, it seems I've been volunteered as your chauffeur. Where do you want to go?'

Dee blushed. 'Oh, please don't feel that you have to—just because Mr Thurman said . . .'

'It's all right—really.' A flicker of irritation crossed his brow, and Dee got the distinct impression that here was a man who never did anything he didn't want to.

She cleared her throat. 'Well, I *was* going to get the

bus over to Birchdown,' she said. 'To the racing circuit. But that's probably miles out of your way.'

'No, it isn't,' he said shortly, beginning to walk towards the lift. 'I'll get you there in no time. Quicker than the bus, anyway.'

His car turned out to be a rather smart BMW, which surprised her, though after a quick glance at the number-plate she noted mentally that it was probably second-hand. He's single and self-indulgent, she told herself, silently assessing him. Spends all he earns on cars and —and . . . She stole a glance at him as he concentrated on the flow of traffic. She took a pride in her ability to sum up character on first impressions. He didn't look the boozy kind, and with dress sense like *that* he wasn't out to impress the girls! She thought of the elegantly tailored three-piece suits Bobby wore when he wasn't in racing leathers. Like his bikes, they were the best that money could buy and gave him the masculine appeal that was part of his charisma.

'Worked at Queen Eleanor's long, have you? It's quite a trek from Birchdown. Do you have to make the trip every day?'

Once more the golden eyes swept over her with that insolent appraisal and she felt a stab of resentment. 'No,' she said uncommunicatively. 'Look, it's very kind of you to offer me a lift, but I can easily catch a bus if you drop me off in town.' Silently she cursed Mr Thurman for placing her in this awkward position.

'Look, I've already told you: I'll *take* you there!' His tone was sharp and she turned to look at him, taking in the high cheekbones and strong, determined jaw; the generously moulded mouth that was both sensuous and stubborn at the same time. Suddenly she found herself wondering about him. If it was all right for *him* to ask questions why shouldn't she?

'Maintenance, are you?' she asked.

He shot her a glance, the eyes momentarily startled and off guard, then the corners of his mouth lifted slightly. 'How clever of you! Yes, I suppose you could say that—and you?' He held up one hand. 'No, don't tell me—it has to be catering?'

Dee's hackles rose. 'As a matter of fact . . .' She stopped. What was the point of telling him what she was? *He* wouldn't know what a scrub-nurse was; most likely he'd think it was something to do with mopping floors. 'You're clever too,' she told him caustically. 'Are you starting work at Queen Eleanor's next week?'

'That's right.' He was smiling openly now. 'Look, I've got an idea. The pubs will be open soon. Why don't we have a drink, then you can fill me in on all the hospital gossip.'

She drew in her breath sharply. His nerve certainly took some beating! 'I don't go in much for hospital gossip,' she said stiffly. 'And besides, I don't think my fiancé would like it.'

He raised a cynical eyebrow at her. 'Really? You *do* surprise me. You know, I had you down as the independent type—Women's Lib and all that; the kind of girl who's her own woman. I thought your sort had abandoned fripperies like engagement rings. And as for being slavishly attached to one man . . .' He smiled, the golden eyes glinting triumphantly as he saw that his barb had found its mark. 'I'll ask you again some time,' he told her casually, 'and if it's equality that's bothering you, I'll even let you pay.'

Dee fumed silently. She wouldn't give him the satisfaction of rising to the obvious bait—or of letting him know that he was partly right—she *had* refused to become officially engaged to Bobby, or even to think about marriage while he was still racing. As they left the town behind them she sat staring unseeingly out at the fields and hedges, thinking of Bobby's well-off parents

and their obvious disapproval of her. They too wanted their son to give up his dangerous obsession with racing —settle down to take his father's place in the family business; get married—but *not* to Dee. A nurse, daughter of divorced parents with little in the way of social or financial attributes, was very far from their idea of the ideal daughter-in-law.

'Well, what is it?'

She turned, startled, suddenly aware that the man at the wheel had asked her a question. 'Sorry?'

He shook his head. 'Miles away, weren't you? I just asked you your name. Mine's Greig Meredith, by the way.'

'Dee Latimer,' she told him shortly.

He glanced at her. 'I thought it only polite to introduce myself. I'm sure nice well-brought-up young women like you don't accept lifts from strangers.' Her lips tightened as she stubbornly refused to react to his obvious goad. He added: 'Dee—would that be short for Deirdre?'

'No, Deanne, believe it or not,' she told him reluctantly. 'Awful, isn't it?'

He made no comment, just grinned, which made her feel acutely uncomfortable and somehow oddly at a disadvantage.

As they stopped outside the entrance to the motorcycle circuit at Birchdown he looked at her, one eyebrow raised. 'Don't tell me you're moonlighting! Do you have another job here?'

Irritation sharpened her voice as she replied: 'No, I don't! If you *must* know, I'm meeting my fiancé. I should have been here hours ago—so if you don't mind . . .' She opened the door and began to get out of the car.

He leaned across as she bent back in to retrieve her handbag. She found his face almost touching hers and she jerked her head backwards, bumping it painfully on

the door arch. Tiny points of amber flashed in the hazel eyes as he remarked coolly: 'I always thought that well-brought-up girls said thank you when they were given a lift.'

Dee rubbed her head, avoiding his eyes. 'I—I'm sorry,' she said grudgingly. 'Of course I'm grateful. It was very kind of you. Thank you very much.'

She stood for a moment on the pavement, watching as the powerful car gathered speed and disappeared. He was quite the coolest customer she'd come across—and she had the oddest feeling that she hadn't seen the last of him.

Bobby was on cloud nine. His fair hair was tousled and his face streaked with dust and oil, but the blue eyes were radiant as he told her: 'The bike's a dream, Dee —an absolute bloody marvel! Old Jim has done wonders on it. The last lap timed in at one minute thirty seconds, and that's enough to put me on the front row of the grid. I'm in with a great chance, girl!' His hug lifted her off her feet and left oily smears on her white shirt. He made no mention of the fact that she was late, and she reflected wryly that she needn't have broken her neck to get here; putting up with all that sniping from a hideously chauvinistic maintenance man. And by the radiant expression on Bobby's face he wouldn't have noticed if she hadn't shown up at all!

CHAPTER TWO

It was eleven p.m. when Bobby's bright yellow sports car drew up outside the house close to the hospital where Dee shared a flat. He switched off the engine and turned in his seat to look at her.

'The offer's still open. Come back to the flat for the night,' he invited. 'We haven't had a chance to be alone all evening.'

She shook her head. She felt like asking whose fault it was. Instead she said: 'Better not. I'm on duty in the morning—besides, you need all the sleep you can get. You've had a long day.'

He grinned at her. 'You had plans to keep me occupied, then? I could always catch up on my sleep after you'd left for work in the morning.'

She sighed wearily. 'Don't be childish, Bobby! Anyway, you're expected back at the party at your parents' house. I'd better not keep you.'

He reached out to the hand on the door handle, covering it with his own. 'You're still mad about the party, aren't you? I couldn't help it, you know. It was as much of a surprise to me as it was to you.' The clear cornflower blue eyes gazed innocently into hers. 'I thought it was quite good of the folks to give it for me, considering the way they feel about my racing.' He slipped an arm around her shoulders. 'Come on, Dee, don't be stroppy,' he said, softly persuasive. 'I've had quite a day. Don't spoil it for me. You've had a face as long as a wellington boot all evening!'

'I'm sorry. I've had quite a day too, though,' she told him. She turned to look at him. Sometimes she really believed he was completely amoral. When he had told her about the party at his parents' house he had been apologetic, pretending he thought it a bore. He knew how much she had looked forward to the quiet evening they had planned—a meal at his flat, then a long talk about their future. Yet once they were there he hadn't bothered to conceal the fact that he was enjoying himself immensely, basking in the admiration of all his friends, flirting outrageously with the other girls there—and his mother had seen to it that every one of his ex-girl-friends was invited; notably Geraldine Moore, a stunningly beautiful girl who was making a name for herself in the modelling world. Dee knew that Bobby had once had quite a serious relationship with Geraldine. She had watched them dancing together, a handsome couple, he in his evening dress, laughing and exercising every ounce of his considerable charm; Geraldine, breathtaking in a shimmering white evening gown, laughing up into his face. Dee had felt abandoned and forgotten; obliged to hang around in the background, ignored by Bobby and disregarded by his parents. She reflected that if it hadn't been for Bobby's elder sister Angela, she would have felt acutely uncomfortable. She burned with resentment as she remembered his mother's smug expression when she had gone to say good night.

'What a *pity* you have to leave so early, my dear,' she'd said affectedly, clearly delighted at the prospect of getting rid of her. She had turned to her son. 'Of course you'll want to take Deanne home, but you won't neglect your guests for *too* long, darling, will you?'

Dee swallowed hard at the hurtful memory. 'I'm tired,' she said. 'I'm sorry if I spoilt it for you. I dare say I wasn't in the mood for a party. You'd better get back. Your mother's expecting you—not to mention Geraldine!' She turned again towards the door, but Bobby pulled her back, holding her firmly. One hand cupped her chin as he forced her to look at him.

'Stupid little fool! I had to circulate, you know. Surely you don't expect me to be glued to your side all the time?' He gave her a rueful look. 'Do grow up, love. Can't you stand a little competition? You know it's you I love, after all.'

'You could have fooled *me* tonight!' She shook her head, her throat tight with threatened tears.

Bobby sighed and shook his head at her reproachfully. 'Might as well get used to it, darling. Better take me for what I am or not at all. I've already made promises to you that I wouldn't make to any other woman living! Do you want to make me over completely?'

Dee shook her head unhappily. Right at that moment she didn't know quite what she wanted. Bobby found her lips and kissed her firmly and insistently. 'Pity you won't be there to see me win next week,' he whispered. 'Especially as it's to be my swan-song.'

She looked up at him, her resentment dissolving a little. 'You *really* mean it, then? You'll really give it all up—just for me—for us?'

'Seems it's the only way you'll marry me, so I've no choice, have I, darling?' he said lightly. He kissed her again, then patted her cheek. 'Right then, if you're not coming home with me I'd better be getting back. See you.'

'When?' Dee asked him. 'I have three days off coming up after tomorrow, remember? Could we spend some time together?'

He frowned. 'I don't know, love. I have an awful lot of practice to get in before the big day—and some more work to do on the bike. There are still a few kinks to iron out.' He grinned. 'I'll try, though—if not I'll make it up to you after the race. I'll ring you some time. All right?'

She stood forlornly on the pavement, watching him

drive away. *Would* she see him during her time off? She
doubted it. Once he became engrossed in working on the
bike he probably wouldn't remember to ring her either.
If he had asked her again; if he had cared enough to use
his own particular brand of persuasion, she might have
changed her mind about going back to his flat—but
he hadn't given her a second chance. Was it her
imagination, or had he seemed almost relieved?'

Wedgwood House was Edwardian and stood in a row of
others in the street behind Queen Eleanor's Hospital.
Once a splendid 'gentlemen's residence', it was now
owned by the local health authority and converted into
five flats, mainly occupied by housemen and senior
nursing staff. Dee climbed wearily to the top floor where
she shared what was unofficially known as the 'Birds'
Nest' with her friend Claire Thompson, who was the
newly appointed Sister on Intensive Care at QE.

She found her flatmate with her feet up in front of the
television. She wore a blue woollen dressing gown and
was sipping coffee from a large mug. She looked up in
surprise as Dee came in.

'You're early! I didn't expect you till . . .' She
grinned. 'Well, let's just say I didn't expect you.' The
smile left her face as she noticed Dee's depressed expression. 'Oh-oh. What's up? You haven't had *another*
row?'

Dee sighed and dropped into a chair. 'Nothing so
satisfying! We had a really tough shift on Theatre One.
An emergency came up just before we were due to
finish, so I didn't get to the circuit till they were almost
ready to go home. Then, instead of the quiet evening
we'd planned, Bobby's parents had laid on a party.'

'And you weren't in the mood?' asked Claire.

Dee shrugged. 'It wasn't that so much. I just seemed
totally out of step with them all. All Bobby's glamorous

ex-girl-friends were invited—I hadn't anything suitable to wear . . .' She threw up her hands. 'It—it was just a disaster from beginning to end.' She gulped hard, and Claire nodded sympathetically.

'She did it on purpose, I suppose—his mother, I mean?' Dee's expression gave her the answer and she sighed. 'Are you sure you know what you're doing, Dee? She's out to wreck it, you know. And do you honestly think Bobby'll give up racing?'

Dee looked up. 'He's promised he will after he's won the Grand Prix.'

'And if he *doesn't* win it?'

Dee stared at her friend. It was a possibility she hadn't even considered. Bobby was so confident that he'd win—so *sure*, especially now that he'd ironed out the problems with the V4.

'Maybe I've a nasty suspicious nature, but he might lose the race just to stall.' Claire held up her hand. 'Oh, I don't mean he'd necessarily do it on purpose. It could even be a subconscious reaction. Racing obviously means an awful lot to him, Dee. I'm sorry, but I just can't see him giving it up that easily.' She looked hard at her friend. 'Look, put yourself in his place. Would you give up nursing?'

Dee's voice was shrill with frustration and tiredness. 'Do you think I haven't asked myself that a hundred times?' She got up to move restlessly round the room. 'You think I'm asking too much of him, don't you?'

Claire shook her head. 'I don't know, love. Maybe Bobby won't be the same person without racing. Maybe those awful smelly, *lethal* machines are what he needs to make him what he is. That's what I'm trying to say. And after all, what was it that made you fall for him in the first place?'

Dee let out her breath in a long sigh and sank into her chair again. 'All I really know for sure is that I couldn't

stand never knowing whether he was going to come home smashed up—living with the anxiety of it. When you've seen as many broken bodies as I have in the theatre . . .' She turned large desperate eyes on her friend. 'It's only because I *love* him, don't you see?'

'Is it?' Claire asked quietly. 'Is that really all of it?' She looked at Dee for a long moment. 'Forgive me, love, but sometimes I wonder if it's the sharing that you can't face—the competition.' Seeing her friend's expression she frowned and shook her head. 'Oh, look, don't get me wrong—*I* couldn't either. Heaven knows, when I meet the man of my dreams *I'll* want him all to myself. Every woman has a right to expect that. It's just that with Bobby I have a feeling . . .' She got up from her chair and walked towards the kitchen. 'Look, I'll make you some coffee. As usual I've opened my big mouth too wide!'

But deep down Dee was only too aware of the unacceptable truth at the heart of Claire's remarks—she knew also that she made them as a friend of long standing who really cared, which, in a way, made them even harder to bear. If they'd been said bitchily they could have been dismissed out of hand. As it was . . . she picked up a magazine and began to leaf through it. Once she and Bobby were married everything would be all right, she told herself desperately. Of course it would. It *had* to be.

'Tell me about your day,' she prompted as Claire sat down opposite her ten minutes later, a pot of freshly brewed coffee on the table between them. She wasn't going to take a chance on the other girl bringing up the subject of Bobby again.

Claire shrugged. 'Things are quiet on IC at the moment. A couple of facial surgery cases and an RTA case who'll be ready to go down to the general ward tomorrow. Just as well as I'm off for the weekend. I always feel guilty, taking time off when we're busy. It's ages since I went home, though. I've almost forgotten what my parents look like!' She looked at her friend over the rim of her cup. 'How about you?'

'It wasn't too bad until just before the shift was over,' Dee told her. 'Then we had the emergency I told you about—an appendicectomy. It proved a little tricky. By the time I got to Birchdown they were almost ready to go home.' She bit her lip. She'd done her best to get Claire off the subject of Bobby and now here she was moving in that direction again herself! 'Mr Thurman organised a lift for me with some maintenance man he was talking to in his room,' she added quickly. 'I just happened to mention that I was late for an appointment and before I knew what was happening he'd fixed it all up. You know what he's like.'

Claire laughed. 'Do I not! Could have been embarrassing for you.'

Dee nodded. 'It was, a bit. I tried to get out of it, but the man insisted. I didn't know what to talk to him about, and to make matters worse he asked me to have a drink with him.'

Claire cocked an enquiring eyebrow. 'Oh! Nice?'

Dee pulled a face. 'Not really. A bit bolshie, especially when I told him I was engaged.'

Claire smiled wryly. 'You can be a bit formidable, you know. You probably put on your Outraged Staff Nurse face. I take it he was suitably chastened?'

'Not a bit of it! After that he seemed to be totally dedicated to putting me down,' Dee told her. 'I hope I don't see too much of *him* around the hospital.'

'Well, I don't suppose you will up in Theatre.' Claire refilled their cups. 'Talking of which—I was introduced to the new orthopaedic consultant this afternoon. Mr Grainger brought him up to look at the RTA case. He's quite an improvement on Grizzly.' She reverted to the nickname the girls had given the elderly orthopaedic consultant in their student days.

Dee laughed, thinking of Mr Grainger's long face and lugubrious manner. '*That* wouldn't be difficult,' she remarked.

'This one's quite a hero, if rumour is to be believed,' Claire went on, warming to her subject. 'Maggie Clark, Grizzly's secretary, told me he'd previously worked in a Sussex hospital and had been involved in treating some of the victims of the Brighton bombing—worked a minor miracle on the spine of a rather well-known MP with some rather nifty micro-surgery, so I heard.'

Dee pulled a face. 'Which means he's probably unbearably conceited by now.'

Claire pursed her lips. 'Just the opposite, by all accounts. It seems he could have had his pick of a dozen jobs, with plenty of opportunities of private patients, but he chose to come to Queen Eleanor's.''

Dee shrugged. 'Personally, I don't trust those over-modest types.'

'I wouldn't say he was that exactly. I'd say he had quite a strong personality, from what I saw,' said Claire. 'Rumour has it that he's a bit of a socialist. All for the underdog—that kind of thing. Anyway, you know what hospital gossip is. You can usually take it with a pinch of salt.'

Dee stretched and stood up. 'Lord save me from do-gooders! They're usually impossibly self-righteous.' She yawned. 'Well, I'm off to bed. I've had enough for one day. Just think—one more day and we shall both have three whole days off. Bliss! I don't know about you, but I can hardly wait.'

The following day was as busy as ever in theatre. A man from the local glass factory was rushed in with fragments of molten glass in his eye; a teenage victim of an accident had crushed ribs, one of which had punctured a lung, a middle-aged man whose spleen had ruptured when he had been involved in an accident at work. Although the time went quickly, Dee was grateful when the hands of the clock moved round to two o'clock—time to hand over to the afternoon shift. She hadn't slept at all well the previous night, mainly because of some of the things Claire had said. Long after she had heard the church clock strike one she had lain awake, worrying about her relationship with Bobby and wondering if she was doing the right thing in trying to get him to give up racing. Deep inside, something Claire had said kept echoing persistently: *Maybe Bobby wouldn't be the same person without his racing. Maybe those smelly, lethal bikes are what makes him what he is.* Of course there was more to Bobby's character than that, she told herself firmly. Once he got down to his job in the family business —took more of the responsibility, he'd change—grow up. Of course he would—*wouldn't he?* It must have been at least three o'clock when she finally fell into an exhausted, over-deep sleep, and when the alarm clock wakened her it had taken every ounce of discipline to drag herself out of bed to go on duty. But at least in the theatre she had had no time to dwell on the disturbing doubts that chased endlessly round in her head.

Mr Thurman, who had removed the ruptured spleen, raised his head to look at his assisting houseman. 'Right then, you can finish off, Mason.' He glanced at the anaesthetist. 'How are things your end?'

The anaesthetist nodded, one eye on his monitor. 'He's fine. I'm glad you've finished, though. He's beginning to show the first signs of stress.'

The surgeon stepped backwards, peeling off his gloves and pulling his mask down. He glanced at Dee as she passed suture materials to Gerald Mason, his houseman.

'Did you manage to keep your appointment on time yesterday, Nurse?'

She nodded. 'Yes, thank you, sir.'

'Good!' He turned to Sister Fairchild, who had been distinctly cool with him this morning. 'All right if I make myself a cup of coffee in your kitchen, Sister?' he asked hesitantly.

She nodded stiffly. 'Certainly, Mr Thurman. I'm sure you know where everything is.'

The patient was transferred to a trolley and wheeled away to the recovery room, and Dee began the routine of counting instruments and checking them off against her list, Sister double-checking with her. Dee glanced at her. 'You're not going to make his coffee for him, then?'

Sister Fairchild sniffed behind her mask. 'No, I'm not. You were right yesterday—I must have looked a complete fool to you all. It isn't part of my job to wait on Douglas Thurman, and I've made up my mind not to do it any more.'

Dee looked up in surprise. She'd never heard Sister use that tone when talking of her adored Douglas Thurman. She actually seemed to mean it too!

On the steps of the hospital Dee paused to take a deep breath of the fresh air. It had been a wet spring and although it was already late May, summer seemed in no hurry to put in an appearance. But today the air smelled good to Dee after the heaviness of the atmosphere in the theatre. Even the most efficient air-conditioning system couldn't clear the hot airlessness that dried up the throat and nasal membranes. Nor could it lighten the inevitable feeling of tension that stretched the nerves, especially after a long and arduous shift. She looked around at the scarlet and yellow tulips blazing in the forecourt flower beds, appreciating their vitality and colour. Three blessed days off! What would she do with them? Surely

Bobby would find *some* time to share with her; he had to have some relaxation, after all.

It was only a short walk back to the flat, and when she got in she made herself a sandwich, then took a long, leisurely bath and washed her hair. Wrapped in her dressing gown and with a towel wound round her damp hair, she went through to the kitchen and dialled Bobby's number on the wall-mounted telephone. There was no reply. She tried the office and got his father's secretary, who told her Bobby had looked in briefly, then gone off for the day. Dee replaced the receiver with a sigh. It looked as though she would just have to wait until he rang her. She decided to use the rest of the afternoon doing some of the little jobs she and Claire never had time for around the flat, and busied herself with duster and vacuum. In the hall cupboard a large pile of ironing awaited her attention. She hated ironing, but at last, feeling very noble, she dragged out the ironing board and set it up in the kitchen, unwinding the iron's flex and plugging it in. Five minutes later when she had finished drying her hair she went back and lifted it, testing the heat with a wetted forefinger. It was stone cold.

'Damn!' They really must invest in a new iron. This one was always letting them down—that was why the pile of ironing was so vast! She slammed it down again. Now she would have to go and see if she could borrow an iron from one of the other tenants—that was if she could find one who wasn't either asleep or on duty! She dressed hurriedly in an old pair of jeans and a sweatshirt, then ran down to the flat on the floor below where Hilda French, the charming middle-aged obstetrician, lived; the girls had borrowed her iron before. But her knocking brought no response. Obviously Hilda was on duty. Dee was just about to go back upstairs when from below the sound of someone whistling floated up. She turned and began to walk down the stairs, following the sound.

The ground floor flat had, until recently, been occupied by one of the junior housemen, but he had married and moved out a couple of weeks ago. Dee had thought the flat was still empty. When she reached the ground floor, however, she saw that the door stood open and the whistling was coming from inside. Peering in, she saw that dust-sheets covered the furniture, which was pushed into the centre of the living room. A man wearing brown overalls stood on a pair of steps in the middle of the living room, whistling happily as he painted the ceiling. His back was towards her. Her spirits lifted. Just what she was looking for—a handyman. Couldn't be better.

'Sorry to trouble you,' she began, 'but my iron has gone wrong. Do you think you could come and have a look at it, please?'

He stopped painting to turn and look at her. 'Oh, hello, it's you again.'

Dee's heart sank. It was that fresh maintenance man who had given her a lift yesterday. If she'd seen it was him she would have crept away unnoticed. She began to back away, shaking her head. 'Oh—look, I don't want to take you away from your work. Don't bother, it's probably beyond repair anyway.'

But he had already climbed down from the steps and was wiping his hands on a cloth. 'No trouble. Just lead me to it,' he said with a smile.

Up in the flat he asked for a screwdriver and removed the sole plate from the iron, peering at it with concentration. 'Ah—I see. There's a loose connection,' he announced. 'Soon have that fixed.' He glanced around. 'Nice little place you have up here. I didn't know they let catering staff have these flats. I thought they were only for medicos.'

'Oh, did you?' Dee said coolly. 'Look, will that take long? Only I've got a pile of ironing to get through.'

He nodded. 'Won't take a jiffy.' He glanced pointedly at his watch and raised an eyebrow at her. 'It's almost four. Time for tea, wouldn't you say?'

She narrowed her eyes, tempted to come back at him with a spiky reply, then she remembered that she was relying on him to mend the iron. She had taken him away from his work downstairs too. Better at least be polite. Without a word she went into the kitchen and put the kettle on, her lips pressed into a tight line. Twice in two days she had found herself beholden to this insolent man.

By the time she had made the tea he had mended the iron and put away the screwdriver in the drawer he had seen her take it from. He seated himself at the kitchen table, looking completely relaxed and at home. Dee poured the tea, looking at him enquiringly.

'Milk and sugar?'

He looked at her, his head on one side. 'I don't suppose you've got any lemon?'

She glanced up at him sharply. Was he being funny? But no, his face was completely innocent. 'You suppose right,' she said shortly.

'Oh—pity.'

She hesitated. 'I—think there's one of those plastic ones in the fridge. Do you want me to look?'

He gave her a wry grin. 'God save me from plastic lemons! No, just a dash of milk will be fine.' She obliged, and he sipped the tea appreciatively. 'Mmm, that's good. I've been working on that ceiling since nine o'clock. Shouldn't think it had been painted for years.'

'Well, now that we have such an enthusiastic main-tenance man around the place who knows—perhaps even *this* flat will get decorated,' said Dee, raising her own cup.'

He looked round the kitchen with a critical eye.

'Mmm, it is a bit grotty, isn't it? But if you want it doing why not do it yourself?' he asked.

She stared at him. 'You're obviously not aware of the kind of hours that cooks work,' she admonished. 'Apart from the fact that our work is so tiring that often all we can do is to fall into bed when we come off duty!'

He shook his head 'Ah, rather you than me. Still, you'll be saying goodbye to all that soon, won't you?'

She frowned and raised an eyebrow at him. 'Saying goodbye? I don't follow.'

'When you get married,' he reminded her. 'When is the happy day, by the way?'

She bridled. 'I—we haven't set a date yet.'

It was his turn to raise an eyebrow. 'Really? Why is that?'

Dee rose from the table and began to rattle the cups pointedly. 'I'll drop you a postcard when we've decided,' she said acidly. 'Thank you for fixing the iron, but don't let me keep you from your work!'

He smiled and leaned back in his chair, folding his arms and crossing one leg over the other. 'Not at all. There's no hurry. As for the postcard—just make it an invitation. I love weddings.' He laughed. 'It must be the sadist in me!'

She opened her mouth, then closed it again. The man really had the most *incredible* nerve! She was about to tell him so when the telephone began to ring. She started. It must be Bobby, but how could she talk to him with this man sitting there listening? Surely he'd have the tact to go. He didn't. The telephone continued to shrill insistently.

'Your phone is ringing,' he told her.

'Yes, I know. I'm not deaf!' She took a step towards it, raising an eyebrow at him. 'You'll have to excuse me. Er—thanks again for mending the iron.'

Unconcerned, he reached across the table to feel the

teapot. 'Not at all. Go ahead, don't mind me,' he said as he poured himself another cup.

Feeling murderous. Dee lifted the receiver. 'Hello?'

'Dee, it's me, Bobby. Dad's secretary said you wanted me.'

'No—I mean, yes. I tried to get you earlier.'

'Anything special?'

'N—no—I just wanted to talk—to see if you were going to be free.' Dee caught the eye of the man sitting at the table. He gave her an encouraging wink. She turned her back abruptly and lowered her voice. 'Look, I can't really talk now . . .'

'Neither can I, as it happens,' Bobby replied quickly. 'Listen, Dee, I was going to ring you later, but I might as well tell you now. We've got quite a tight schedule over the next few days, and I can't see myself getting a minute free. Of course, you *could* come over to the circuit if you like—or to the garage,' he added doubtfully.

Dee's heart sank. Even if Bobby had sounded as though he wanted her there, the prospect of spending her precious time off hanging around a grimy garage was hardly what she had visualised. 'Surely you can find an hour or two,' she said plaintively. 'We've hardly seen each other these past few weeks.'

'It's only till after the race,' he reminded her.

There was a lot she wanted to say, but already she could hear Bobby talking abstractedly to someone in the background. Besides which, she was still acutely aware of the toffee-brown eyes of the man at the table, fixed firmly on her back. 'All right,' she said helplessly. 'I'll see you when I see you, I suppose.'

'I'll make it up to you, love—promise.' Although Bobby was still speaking to her she knew that in his mind he was already back with his beloved bike. Her shoulders drooped. What was the use?

'Goodbye.' Almost before the word her left her lips

she heard the 'clunk' of the receiver being dropped back on to its rest as Bobby hung up. She felt abandoned —dismissed—a chore to be quickly dealt with and forgotten. Sick with disappointment, she stood staring at the buzzing telephone in her hand, the man sitting at the table momentarily forgotten until his voice reminded her of his presence.

'Boy-friend?'

She turned to look at him. 'Oh—yes.'

'You look shattered. Did he . . . ?'

'He's a motorcycle racer—riding in the Grand Prix next week,' she told him. 'He's going to be busy during the next few days. I—I had hoped we might spend some time together. I've got three days off, you see.' *Why was she telling him all this?* She didn't have to explain. It was just the way he was looking at her.

'Too bad,' he said sympathetically. 'Look, it's just an idea, but why don't you get on and paint this kitchen? Nothing like keeping busy to kill time. I'll give you a hand if you like. As it happens, I'm free this weekend too.'

Dee opened her mouth to refuse, then suddenly changed her mind. She had nothing else to do, so why not? At least it would be a more productive way of spending her time off than hanging around a draughty garage or a noisy racing circuit, and it wasn't every day she got the offer of free professional help. 'All right, you're on,' she said. 'Will you get the paint or shall I?'

CHAPTER THREE

'WELL, that's the first coat on. I think we deserve a break, don't you?' Greig straightened his back and glanced across at Dee as she put the last few brush strokes to the wall she was painting.

'I agree.' She groaned a little as she straightened her back. 'I'm new to this kind of exercise. I've a terrible feeling I'm going to ache all over tomorrow,' she told him.

They had been working on the kitchen all day and Dee noticed with surprise that it was now almost seven o'clock. Neither of them had eaten anything since a snatched sandwich at lunchtime, and suddenly she felt guilty. 'You must be ravenous! I should have cooked something,' she remarked.

He gave her the wry grin she was growing used to. 'Why should you? You've worked as hard as I have. Besides, it isn't easy with the kitchen upside-down.'

'Yes, but it *is* my flat—and you're working for nothing in your own time. Fair's fair,' she said. 'Look, give me time to clean up and I'll do us some beans on toast or something, right?'

He grimaced. 'I never could stand beans on toast! Tell you what, I'll take you out for a pub snack.' When he saw her hesitating he added, 'You can pay if you like.'

She laughed, wiping the paint from her hands with a paper towel. 'All right, it's a deal. Just give me twenty minutes.'

Twenty minutes later they were sitting in the bar of the Fiddlers Three, a rather trendy pub on the outskirts of

Middlehurst. Dee hadn't wanted to go to the Danish Invader, where most of the hospital staff usually congregated. Being seen with Greig might be embarrassing and difficult to explain when her friends all knew she was engaged to Bobby.

As they settled themselves by a window overlooking the patio, with their drinks and chicken-in-the-basket, Greig looked at her. She had slipped hurriedly into a pair of cream cord jeans and a black angora sweater before coming out, and although she had applied a hasty dash of lipstick, she still wore her hair in the short, stiff plait she had adopted for working.

'You know, you look about twelve with your hair like that,' he remarked as he regarded her. 'It's a wonder they let you in here!'

She glanced across at him as he took a long grateful pull at his beer. This time yesterday a remark like that would have stung her to a hasty, indignant retort, but she was becoming used to his frank and direct way of speaking. Maybe it was something to do with his being Welsh, she told herself. She gave him a sidelong glance. He still wore the jeans he had been working in, yet, unlike her own, there wasn't a speck of paint on them. That was professionalism for you! He'd thrown the brown leather blouson over his white, short-sleeved tee-shirt and his wiry brown hair looked as tousled as ever. She couldn't imagine it ever lying smooth. She'd also noticed that he had the most extraordinary hands —broad and strong, the fingers long and supple, the nails well manicured. He was obviously the kind of man who had to shave twice a day. At the moment his cheeks were quite dark and rough. Odd—he was the only man she had ever known who managed to look attractive with stubble! He caught her looking at him and the hazel eyes twinkled.

'What's up—paint on my nose?'

She blushed and shook her head. 'No. I was just wondering why on earth you chose to spend your free time helping me to decorate. It's a bit of a busman's holiday for you, isn't it?'

He shrugged. 'Call it my innate chivalry. I never could turn a blind eye to a damsel in distress,' he told her, tucking into his chicken.

'I wouldn't say I was exactly "in distress",' she told him. 'More at a loose end. Anyway, it's good of you, and I'm grateful.'

He glanced up at her. 'By the way, how old *are* you?' he asked with a directness that took her breath away.

'What's that got to do with anything?' she asked.

He shrugged. 'Nothing, except what I was saying earlier—about your looking twelve.'

'I'm definitely older than twelve,' she told him evasively.

'Good God, you're not one of those women who's cagey about her age, are you?' he asked in surprise.

'Not at all!'

He chewed thoughtfully for a moment, then said: 'I'm thirty-six.'

'Congratulations!'

He gave her a lopsided grin. 'Go on, tell me—or do you want me to play guessing games?'

Dee laid down her fork for a moment. 'Well, I've been at QE since I was eighteen . . .' She was about to mention her training and subsequent career, then she remembered that she was supposed to be on the catering staff and said instead: 'That was five years ago—work it out for yourself.'

He winced. 'You make me feel about a hundred! So you've been here all that time? Never wanted to move on?' When she shook her head he added: 'Ah yes, the speed king—what's his name, Bobby?—kept you here. Only natural, I suppose.'

She watched him eat for a moment, then made up her mind to ask: 'What about you—aren't you married?'

He stopped, his fork halfway to his mouth; his eyes slightly startled as they looked at her. 'Why do you ask that?'

'Why not?' she countered. 'You seem to feel free to ask *me* personal questions.'

Greig nodded. 'Fair enough.' He dabbed his mouth with the paper napkin and leaned back. 'What do you think—do I look married?'

She frowned. 'I don't know. Not specially. Are you?'

'I suppose you could call me married, yes,' he said after a pause.

She laughed. 'What kind of an answer is that?'

He didn't join in her laughter. 'It's the only way I can describe it really. We've been separated for the past two years—and it's a situation that isn't likely to alter.'

Dee bit her lip, looking down at her food. She had obviously touched him on a raw spot, and now she wished she hadn't asked. 'Oh—I'm sorry.' There was a small, awkward silence, then she asked: 'What about your family—I mean your parents—brothers and sisters?'

Greig looked up, his face brightening. 'I'm not short of those. They're all in Wales. Dad, four brothers and a sister. I came roughly in the middle. Three of them are in teaching, two in industry. My mother died five years ago. She was a Scot, which is where I get my Christian name from, but Dad still potters around quite happily in his greenhouse. He was a dyed-in-the-wool coalminer —started down the pit when he was fourteen and stayed there until an accident back in 1965 robbed him of the use of his legs.'

Dee stared at him. 'Oh!—Oh, how awful. I'm sorry.'

He smiled. 'No need. He doesn't bear any grudges, and when we're not around he has plenty of good friends who make sure he has everything he wants.' He spread.

his hands. 'So that's my potted biography.' He tossed the ball back at her: 'Your turn now.'

She took a deep breath. 'Well, let's see—my mother and father divorced soon after I left school,' she told him. 'Mum remarried quite soon after and went to Canada. Dad met someone else two years ago—a girl only five years older than me. Ever since then he's taken on a new lease of life—holidays abroad, a new house —he's even taken up dancing again.' She couldn't quite keep the resentment out of her voice as she added: 'Ridiculous at his age, isn't it?'

'I don't know. How old is he?'

'Forty-seven.'

He gave her a quizzical grin. 'Hardly over the hill, is it?' When she looked doubtful he went on: 'Put it this way, I wouldn't like to think of myself as past it in eleven years from now!'

Dee found herself blushing. 'Oh, I didn't mean—no, of course not . . .'

He laughed at her confusion. 'Would I be right in thinking that you're not totally in favour of your prospective ma-in-law?'

She looked at him askance. 'Good God, I don't see her as *that*!' She lifted her glass of white wine and fiddled with the stem. 'I just don't want Dad to be hurt, that's all. I don't much care for the way she's changed him either.'

'You're close?' She looked up to find him looking searchingly at her and looked away again.

'We were.'

'So you see her more as a rival for your dad's affection than as a stepmother?'

Dee took a deep breath. All this was getting much too heavy. What was it about this man that could draw out her innermost thoughts – the ones she didn't want to think? Who did he think he was—a psychiatrist? 'I'm not *that* immature,' she protested. Looking up, she found the penetrating hazel eyes still on her and she asked: 'Does your wife live in Wales too?'

A muscle twitched in his cheek. 'No. In London,' he said briefly.

'So what went wrong?' She was determined to give him a dose of his own medicine, but he saw through her subterfuge and shook his head at her, the golden eyes twinkling.

'Okay, so I overdid the shrink bit.' He held up crossed fingers. 'Pax. I won't probe your wounds if you don't probe mine. All right?'

'All right.'

They finished their meal in silence. Greig drained the last of his beer and looked enquiringly at her. 'Another?'

She shook her head. 'No, thanks, I've had enough. What now? Do we go back to work, or won't the first coat be dry enough yet?'

He looked doubtful. 'Better give it until the morning —unless you've something else planned for tomorrow, that is?'

'No, nothing.' She looked up at him with challenging eyes. 'You know damned well I haven't anything planned, don't you? You heard every word that was said on the phone yesterday.'

He stared at her incredulously. 'You mean you never do *anything*—go anywhere your beloved Bobby doesn't go? Haven't you any other friends—interests?'

She felt her colour rising again and her eyes flashed like emeralds as she said accusingly: 'You're doing it *again*!'

He held up his hands. 'Sorry. It just seems rather a waste, that's all.' He stood up. 'Shall we go, then?'

Outside in the car park he looked at her. 'I'll take you home.'

Dee nodded. 'Thanks.'

Outside Wedgwood House Greig switched off the engine and turned to look at her. 'Am I invited up for a nightcap?'

She shook her head firmly. 'Sorry, no nightcap.'

'Not even a cup of coffee?' He looked outraged and disappointed, and she hesitated. He *was* helping her decorate the kitchen, and even after what he had said about the bar snack being on her he had insisted on paying for it and the drinks himself. Coffee was the least she could offer in return. Besides, she didn't want to give him the satisfaction of supposing she suspected his intentions. Once more he had her at the disadvantage, damn him!

'Oh, all right,' she said, opening the door and swinging her feet out on to the pavement. 'One coffee and a biscuit, that's all you get. Then I'm for an early night.'

Upstairs as she made coffee in the kitchen she watched through the open door as he prowled round the living room, peering at the photographs and small ornaments the girls had displayed about the room. He was what her mother would have called a 'fine figure of a man' —about five eleven, she guessed, with broad shoulders and a powerful-looking chest. She supposed that must be due to all the physical work he did. The tight white tee-shirt he wore revealed strong, round biceps and the rippling muscles of his back as he bent forward to study a framed snapshot of Claire that stood on the coffee table.

'That's Claire, my flatmate,' Dee called to him. 'She's away for the weekend. The kitchen'll be a surprise for her when she gets back.' As she waited for the milk to heat she found herself wondering about Greig's wife. Was she beautiful—had she been unfaithful? Had he? Or were they simply incompatible? How long had the marriage lasted? she wondered. And was he still in love with her? What *was* it that made people part after loving each other enough to share their lives? She'd never understood quite what went wrong with her parents' marriage.

'Smells good. I love the scent of freshly made coffee.' His voice from the doorway made her jump and she noticed just in time that the milk was boiling, rising quickly up the sides of the saucepan with a hissing sound. *'Oh!'* She hastily turned off the gas and snatched at the hot handle of the pan.

'Watch it!' He stepped forward and caught her arm, steadying her as the milk slopped over. 'Don't want you scalding yourself all on my account!' He took the pan from her and poured the milk deftly into the waiting jug, then turned to the sink to run water into the pan.

'Domesticated too!' she remarked. 'Is there no end to the man's talents, I ask myself?'

'A case of having to, these past two years,' he said. 'But don't you worry, if I could find a nice obliging *and* attractive little woman to attend to my needs I'd give it up tomorrow!' He glanced round at her, a wicked smile lifting the corners of his mouth. 'A penny for the thoughts you were having just then. You were looking very pensive.'

Dee busied herself putting cups on to a tray and getting the biscuit tin down from the cupboard. She was *almost* sure he could read her thoughts! Must be all that Celtic blood! 'If you must know, I was wondering what makes marriages go wrong,' she told him with ice-cool honesty. 'Though in view of that last remark I'd guess that in your case it had something to do with that inbuilt chauvinism of yours!' She picked up the tray and turned to him with a defiant look. 'There—wish you hadn't asked?'

His face broke into a broad grin. 'Deanne Latimer, you're quite a girl!'

He drank his coffee quite quickly, then to her surprise he stood up and stretched. 'Well, you want an early night, so I'll go.'

She looked up at him as he towered above her. Suddenly, without quite knowing why, she was reluctant to.

see him go—knew that when he had gone the flat would seem strangely empty. But she got to her feet without comment. 'Right. See you in the morning, then?'

He shook his head. 'You're forgetting—I have to work tomorrow. But if you'd like to leave it till the evening . . .'

She shook her head. 'No, I wouldn't dream of it. I can easily manage the second coat myself. Silly of me to forget that you had to work.' She held out her hand. 'Thanks for all your help.'

Greig grasped the hand she offered and for a moment they stood, looking at each other, then he reached out his other hand and touched her cheek lightly with one finger. 'I dare say your Bobby will be round to see you tomorrow anyway.' He smiled. 'Goodnight.'

On the pavement downstairs Greig Meredith paused to look up at the small square of yellow light that was Dee's window. What the hell was a girl like that doing, getting herself involved with a man immature enough to be tearing round a track on a motorbike? Even without meeting Bobby Carr it was clear to Greig that he'd only make her unhappy. During his inspection of the living room he'd seen a snapshot of him on the mantelpiece, taken obviously after a win at the track; a wreath of flowers round his neck and the traditional bottle of champagne spurting foam in his hands. He had conceit and self-indulgence written all over him. Dee was the sort of girl who needed a secure kind of love—a man she could rely on. She was neither weak, nor a fool—plenty of spirit there—yet she had an essential femininity, a touching vulnerability that made him feel a protective anger for the thoughtless lout who could let her down and disappoint her without a second thought. He felt in his pocket for his car keys, shaking his head impatiently. He was a fine one to be getting himself involved in other people's love-lives; criticising people for their choice of partners! He of all people had no right after the disaster that was his own marriage!

He got into the car and slid the key into the ignition, his thoughts drifting back to Heather; cool, beautiful, sophisticated Heather with her long legs and her silky dark hair. He'd been flattered, if he was honest with himself—flattered that a girl like that should fall for him, a poor medical student, the son of a Welsh coalminer from the valleys, when it was obvious that she could have had her pick of any man in London. He'd been dazzled, yes, that was the word. Too blind to see that her motives had nothing to do with love and that it wasn't the man that attracted her, but the status. Heather had fondly imagined that being married to an ambitious doctor would give her the key to the social circles she'd always wanted to belong to. And when she had discovered that his ambition was primarily to heal and cure rather than to rise to the top of the heap—that the long hours he spent in the theatre and at the hospital were for the benefit of others and not for her, she was devastated. She'd felt cheated. She'd accused him of being a sham —called him a fake—and a lot of other things too; cruel, bitter, ugly things he'd never have believed her capable of. *'Were you really so conceited that you thought you could leave me alone for nights on end and still find me patiently waiting with your slippers by the fire when you deigned to come home?'* He could still hear the shrill, mocking words she had flung at him when the showdown had finally come and he had found her in the arms of another man. He shook his head as though to rid himself of the painful memory. All that was over and done with. Soon his divorce would be through and Heather would be married to her new love, a wealthy business man who would give her all the things she'd missed out on.

Sitting in the car, he found himself examining his

motives for allowing Dee to remain ignorant about his identity. Could it have had something to do with his past experience? Had he perhaps wanted to see if there was a woman who would accept him for himself alone? He sighed. Heather must have dented his ego more deeply than he had thought. Until two days ago he hadn't even looked at another woman—hadn't had the slightest interest—and now? He revved the engine and nosed the car out into the road, smiling slightly as he remembered the way Dee had stubbornly stuck to her pretence too. She couldn't know, of course, that he had seen her earlier when he had watched Douglas Thurman, the general surgeon, at work from the viewing room with Gilbert Grainger, the consultant whose place he was taking. True, most of her face had been covered by mask and cap, but he would have recognised those incredible green eyes anywhere. What, he wondered, were *her* reasons for keeping up the charade?

But Dee Latimer was spoken for, he reminded himself. He drew a deep breath and flexed his shoulders as he turned the car smoothly on to the forecourt of the hotel where he was staying temporarily. Ah well, it was the story of his life! Besides, there was many a slip, so they said!

Wrapped in her dressing gown after her bath, Dee wandered back into the kitchen to stare at the silent telephone on the wall. Bobby hadn't rung—and she had promised herself that she wouldn't ring him. But how could she go to sleep without speaking to him? Had he *really* been working on the bike all this time? Couldn't he have found a few minutes to speak to her on the phone? On a sudden impulse she reached for the receiver and dialled the number of his flat. Tomorrow might be their last chance to spend some time together before his big race. Surely . . .

At the other end the ringing tone went on and on. She replaced the receiver and dialled the number of the garage where he kept the bike; again, no reply. Finally, after a long pause, she made up her mind and dialled the number of his parents' house.

'Hello?' His mother's husky drawl was quite unmistakable.

'Oh, hello, Mrs Carr. It's Dee. Is Bobby there?'

There was a slight pause before Lena Carr said: 'Oh—isn't he with you?'

Dee bit back the impulse to ask if she would have been ringing if he were! 'No. I haven't heard from him all day,' she said.

'Oh dear, he is too bad! I reminded him before he left the party the other night that he'd promised to spend some time with you this weekend.'

Dee closed her eyes. It was Lena's way of reminding her that he'd gone back to the party after taking her home—also that he'd *needed* reminding.

'Of course, it *was* rather late,' Lena went on. 'And his mind was so full of that wretched machine of his, as you know. I don't know if I'll see him, but is there any message you'd like me to pass on if I do?'

'No, not really,' Dee said despondently. 'I shall be back at work the day after tomorrow, so there isn't much point. Good night, Mrs Carr.'

'Good night, dear. And I'm *so* sorry you've been disappointed.' It seemed to Dee that she hardly bothered to conceal the note of triumph in her voice.

She hung up and went through to the bedroom. Only one more day of her break left, and it looked as though she'd be spending that alone. She thought over the day she had just spent, wishing wistfully that Greig didn't have to work tomorrow. To her surprise she found that she had enjoyed his company as well as his help. At least he was a man who kept his word.

CHAPTER FOUR

THERE is only so much satisfaction to be got out of painting a room by oneself, and by the time Dee had applied the second coat to the kitchen walls the following day she had decided that she had exhausted it. As she cleaned up and replaced the table and chairs in their accustomed positions she sighed with satisfaction. Claire would be surprised—pleased too, she hoped. They had been complaining about the state of the place for months now, but had found neither time nor energy to do anything about it. Now, thanks to Greig Meredith, it was done.

She showered and changed into a cotton skirt and tee-shirt, ate a snack lunch, then sat wondering what to do with the rest of the day. Bobby still hadn't rung. She could have tried him again, but she had already decided against it. If he wanted her he knew where she was.

She was washing her few dishes when the telephone rang. Hastily drying her hands, she snatched up the receiver. 'Hello—Bobby?'

'Sorry to disappoint you, love—it's me, Angie. Mother said you rang last night. I've got the day off and I wondered if you'd like to go shopping this afternoon and maybe see a film or something later?'

Dee winced. Bobby's sister meant well, she knew, but she hated people feeling sorry for her. 'No need to worry about me,' she said quickly. 'I've been busy decorating the kitchen while Claire's away for the weekend. 'I've hardly noticed the time slipping by. I really didn't expect to see Bobby anyway. You needn't feel you have to entertain me on his behalf.'

'As it happens, I'd really like to see you.' Angela sounded hurt. 'I'm not being patronising, you know.'

Dee bit her lip. Sometimes she didn't take time to think before she reacted. 'Sorry, Angie,' she said. 'I'd love to go shopping with you, you know that. And of course I've been disappointed not to see Bobby. I get a bit defensive about it, that's all.'

Angie was sympathetic and quick to forget the unintentional sharpness. 'I know, love. Look, I'll pick you up in about half an hour—all right?'

'Fine. I'll look forward to it.'

At thirty, Angela Carr was five years older than her brother. She worked as her father's personal assistant in the small engineering business he had founded twenty years ago and everyone had the greatest respect for her efficiency and the hard work and loyalty she put into the firm. Her father knew only too well that she could run the firm easily on her own, but it was still his dearest wish to see his son Bobby take over from him on his retirement. Watching from the living room window, Dee saw the other girl arrive in her little white sports car and emerge, fresh and well groomed as ever. She wore a tailored grey suit and her short blonde hair shone with health and expert hairdressing. Dee smiled, waving as she saw her glance up towards the window, then she picked up her coat and bag and went to meet her prospective sister-in-law.

Angie chatted as she drove into the town centre, talking about her job, the holiday she had booked for next month—everything, it seemed to Dee, except her brother. The powerful little car climbed to the fourth deck of the multi-storey car park where Angie finally found a space and parked. Then they went off to explore the shops in the huge Galesborough shopping complex. Dee helped Angie choose some holiday clothes, giving her opinions and advice when it was asked for. Angie received an infinitely larger pay cheque each month than she did, but she wasn't envious. She loved her job and knew she wouldn't swap it for Angie's, which involved placating irritable businessmen and keeping tabs on all her father's moves and appointments.

When Angie had made all her purchases she looked enquiringly at Dee. 'What about you? Isn't there anything you want?'

Dee shook her head. 'Strictly speaking I can't really afford anything at the moment.' She smiled. 'If I had a good excuse like you do it would be different, but I haven't.'

'What about the big race?' Angie asked.

'I'm going to be on duty, so I'll have to miss it,' Dee told her. 'As luck would have it I change from the early shift to the late one on that very day!'

'Oh, that's too bad. Couldn't you swap duties with anyone?'

Dee frowned. 'To tell you the truth, I'm almost glad of the excuse not to go,' she confessed. 'I hate watching Bobby race—it terrifies me. I can't see what people get so excited about.'

Angie gave her a wry smile. 'I'm afraid most of the excitement is about what you hate so much—the thrill of the speed and the risks the riders take—and the fear of someone getting hurt too, I'm afraid. I know it's ghoulish, but it's a fact of life.'

Dee shivered. 'I'm a coward, I suppose. I know Bobby would like me to be there.'

Angie shrugged. 'Once he's on that track the rest of us don't exist for him, so I shouldn't worry too much about it,' she said.

'I know, but this race is to be his last. It's all for me that he's giving it up after the Grand Prix, so I feel I should . . .' Dee broke off as she saw the look on the other girl's face. But Angie quickly adjusted her expression.

'Well, if you can't be there, you can't,' she said.
'Nothing to be done about it. And you'll be at the party
afterwards, won't you?'

Dee smiled. 'Naturally.' The get-together on the
evening of the Grand Prix was where they planned to
announce their engagement officially. Naturally she
wouldn't miss that.

'Well then, there's your excuse! You just *have* to have
a new dress!' Angie took her arm firmly. 'And you're
going to have one—even if I have to buy it for you
myself.' She steered Dee determinedly towards her
favourite shop. 'And I don't want to hear another word
from you on the subject—right?'

They spent a pleasant half-hour choosing a dress for
Dee to wear to the party, finally agreeing on a delicious
creation in midnight blue silk, which proved to be at
least twice the price that Dee had intended to spend.
However, Angie insisted that it set off Dee's delicate
colouring dramatically and that she would be *mad* to
pass it up. It might have been made for her. Angie
cajoled and pleaded until at last Dee gave in and bought
the dress, firmly refusing to accept the loan Angie
generously offered. They were still arguing amicably as
they left the shop, and finally Dee agreed to compromise: the other girl could treat her to tea before they
went on to the cinema.

The film was an historical epic that had recently swept
the board of Hollywood awards, and the girls enjoyed it
very much. They were discussing it as they came out of
the cinema when Angie suddenly noticed that she was
missing one of her gloves.

'Could you wait here a minute while I pop back and
look for it?' she looked at Dee apologetically. 'I'm sorry,
I'm always doing this sort of thing. I won't be longer than
I can help.'

'It's all right. Take your time.' Dee stood to one side

as the crowd went past. The cinema had been packed and it was clear that everyone had enjoyed the film. As they passed on their way to the exits she could hear their remarks. Then suddenly her eyes were drawn towards a couple on the other side of the foyer. They were laughing together as they moved towards the exit. The man turned his fair, curly head briefly in Dee's direction and she saw with a shock that it was Bobby—the girl clinging to his arm was Geraldine. With lightning speed it flashed through her mind that if Angie hadn't lost that glove she might never have known—never have seen them. It was sheer coincidence—an ironic twist of fate. They had reached the door now, and Dee watched as Bobby's arm went protectively round the other girl's shoulders as they were jostled by the crowd. A dart of pain went through her. He'd been too busy to ring her, yet he'd found time to take Geraldine to the cinema. *And what else besides?* a small cruel voice goaded inside her head. Hot colour flood her cheeks as the humiliation of it overwhelmed her. She looked around her, feeling suddenly as though everyone in the foyer knew and was looking at her pityingly. In her head Bobby's words echoed: *'Can't you stand a little competition? You know it's you I love.'* Obviously, he thought he had a perfect right to do this sort of thing. Was this the way it would always be? Would she always have to share him—if not with racing then with other women?

'Dee! Are you all right, love?'

She turned to find Angie at her side, looking at her with concern. 'Oh, hello. Did you find your glove?' She forced a smile.

'Yes—it was in my bag all the time. Look, don't you feel well? You look like death!'

Dee was, in fact, trembling now. The warm colour had drained from her cheeks, leaving her deathly pale, but she shook her head. 'I'm fine. Let's go, shall we? Tell you what—why don't you come back to the flat for coffee? Claire will be home by now and you haven't seen her for ages.'

Somehow she got through the rest of the evening, putting on a show of normality for the benefit of Claire and Angie. But as the girls chatted Angie's eyes kept straying thoughtfully to Dee's face. Obviously in the few minutes they had been apart something had happened to upset her. If only she would say what it was! But she didn't probe, knowing that if Dee had wanted to tell her about it, she would have done.

Long after she was in bed Dee lay awake, her eyes wide open. Every time she closed them she saw again the couple at the cinema—the way Bobby's arm lay across the girl's shoulders. The gesture had looked so natural, as though it had happened a hundred times in the past. Then there was the look in Geraldine's eyes as she had laughed up at him, intimate and adoring. Dee had tried to tell herself that the two had, in all probability, met by chance. Perhaps Bobby had rung her here at the flat after she had gone out with Angie, found her out and gone to the cinema by himself. Meeting Geraldine there had simply been a coincidence. But deep in her heart she knew that no such coincidence existed. She longed to talk to someone about it—to be reassured, but she felt too betrayed and humiliated to confide, even in Claire, her oldest friend.

When she reported for duty on the surgical unit the following morning Sister Fairchild had a favour to ask her.

'Oh, Staff, would you mind if I lent you to Theatre Four this morning? Staff Nurse Hall is down with some kind of 'flu bug and it's Mr Grainger's list. He hates changes of any kind, but he knows you.'

Dee nodded. 'Fine. I'll go along and report to Sister right away.'

Mary Fairchild laid a hand on her arm and peered into her face. 'You *are* all right, aren't you? You're looking a bit peaky. I hope you're not going down with this bug that's going around.'

'I'm fine, I promise,' Dee assured her. 'I spent my break decorating, so it wasn't very restful, that's all.'

Sister shook her head. 'You young girls don't get enough sleep. I'm always telling you . . .'

In the nurses' changing room in Theatre Four Dee found Sister rushing around in a flap. When she saw Dee she looked profoundly relieved.

'Oh, thank goodness! It's very good of Sister Fairchild to spare you. I'm short-staffed and I've no one experienced enough to scrub for Mr Grainger.' She lowered her voice. 'You know how fussy and exacting he is. He's bringing his replacement along with him this morning too and I do want to put on a good show. Standards are so important, I feel, don't you?' As Dee began to scrub up Sister scanned the list, chattering on: 'We've got a hip replacement on the list this morning as well as the routine jobs—two cartilage removals—a bad humerus fracture to reset and an osteoma to investigate. I believe the new man will be doing most of it.' She glanced at Dee. 'I expect you've heard about his claim to fame in the Brighton bombing tragedy?'

Dee nodded. Gowned and masked, she moved into the theatre to begin her preliminary work, taking a last look at the list of operations to be performed. 'I did hear something, yes. I just hope he's not going to throw his weight about on the strength of it!'

'Oh, I don't think so. I've only met him briefly, but he seemed very down to earth,' said Sister, following her.

With infinite care, the selection of instruments for the first operation was laid out methodically on the trolley, carefully noted and checked by Dee and one of the other nurses, then covered with a green sterile towel. The anaesthetist arrived along with his technician and they went through a last-minute check of their equipment. Presently Sister put her head round the door to tell them that the surgeons had indicated that they were ready and she had just rung down to the ward. The first patient was on his way up. Dr Brian James, the anaesthetist, went out to meet and prepare him. The morning's list was beginning.

The two surgeons entered the theatre through the door leading to the surgeons' changing room. Both masked and gowned in theatre greens, their gloved hands held up, they took up their positions at the plinth. Although little of their faces was visible, Mr Grainger was easily recognisable from the broad shoulders and shambling bear-like gait that had earned him the nick-name 'Grizzly'. The other man was taller and quite obviously younger. Mr Grainger nodded towards the other surgeon, indicating to Dee that he would be doing the first op, and she moved the trolley into position and lifted the sterile cloth with tongs so that he could see and approve the instruments laid out for his use. She raised her eyes to his for his approval—and almost let out a cry of shocked surprise as she recognised the toffee-brown ones smiling back into hers over the green mask.

The morning's orthopaedic list passed without incident. Dee watched with fascination as the new consultant worked. Everything that was said about him was obviously true—he *was* brilliant. As she watched the last operation of the morning, a delicate one to replace a damaged hip joint with one of metal and plastic, she marvelled at his skill and deftness, remembering that this was a man who had risen from humble beginnings, who had had no help or special privileges. He must have gone without and worked hard to become a surgeon; he must have had a great deal of determination to get where he was at such a relatively early age. But when the morning's work was over she turned briskly towards her own vitally important tasks, avoiding his eyes as she methodically counted the used instruments, checking them off against her list. She heard Mr Grainger warmly congratulate the younger man and invite him to write up the case-notes himself. Without turning she heard the two men leave the theatre, and then, only then, did she allow herself to fume at the way Greig had deceived her. What a good laugh he must have had at her expense! She blushed under her mask as she remembered letting him believe he was right in assuming that she was from the canteen—thinking there was little point in explaining because he wouldn't understand what a scrub-nurse was!

In the changing room the conversation was all about the new consultant, the nurses enthusing over his power-ful build and looks—about the velvet warmth of his Welsh accent. Even Sister simperingly remarked that he reminded her of a young Richard Burton and that she wouldn't mind betting that he could sing too with a voice like that! Well, the Welsh were noted for it, weren't they?

Dee changed and escaped as quickly as she could. Anger always made her hungry. Besides, she'd overslept after her restless night and hadn't had time for more than a slice of toast for breakfast. In the canteen she helped herself to a large helping of shepherd's pie, with treacle pudding to follow, then looked around to find a vacant table. She wasn't in the mood for sharing or making conversation at the moment.

She finally found one on the far side of the room and set out her lunch, but she had barely started when someone stopped by her side and a voice enquired: 'Well? Am I forgiven?'

There was no need to look up—and anyway her face had reddened so much that she couldn't. 'No!' she said,

wincing as she hastily swallowed a mouthful of scalding pie.

Greig took the seat opposite and folded his arms on the table, leaning forward to search her face anxiously. 'You've gone a funny colour.'

'It's the pie—it's hot.' She laid down her knife and fork and looked him straight in the eyes. 'Why did you tell me you were in maintenance?' she asked accusingly.

He laughed. 'Well, first, it was *you* who said that, not me. And secondly, it's true in a way. People maintenance.'

She shook her head. 'It wasn't fair—pretending like that. It was a shock, seeing you in theatre this morning.' Another thought occurred to her and she narrowed her eyes at him. 'And another thing—what were you doing decorating that flat downstairs?'

'It happens to be *my* flat,' he told her simply. 'The last tenant had painted the ceiling brown and I found it rather depressing.'

'Oh.' She applied herself once more to the shepherd's pie, glad to have something on which to turn her attention.

Greig leaned towards her. 'I *could* ask you why you let me believe you were in catering!—but I won't.'

She looked up at the glinting eyes. 'You knew I wasn't!' she accused. 'All the time, you *knew*!'

He held up his hands in mock surrender. 'All right —guilty. I just couldn't resist it.' He smiled. 'May I just say, Staff Nurse Latimer, that you are a *very* efficient scrub-nurse? Always exactly the right instrument at the ready, even before it was asked for—a real professional, if I may say so.'

She grunted: 'Hmmp! Flattery will get you nowhere!'

'It happens to be true. I mean it.' When she didn't answer he asked: 'How's the kitchen? Did you manage to finish it?'

Dee nodded. 'Yes. It looks lovely. My flatmate was really pleased.' She paused, then: 'Thanks—for helping me with it, I mean.'

'It was nothing—only the first coat.'

'No—no, it was all the preparation too, filling up the cracks and so on in the proper professional way. I'd never have managed by myself.'

He grinned. 'I take it we're still mates, then?'

She shrugged. 'If you like.'

'Right. Then how about having a drink with me this evening? If you can stand the muddle in the flat I'll even cook you dinner as a kind of olive branch.' He gave her a challenging look. 'I bet you've never tasted Welsh haggis!'

Dee opened her mouth to refuse, then suddenly she remembered the way Bobby had kept her waiting for a telephone call all weekend while he took Geraldine to the cinema. There seemed little point in waiting around for him now. Why shouldn't she have a drink with Greig? 'All right, you're on,' she said, a hint of defiance in her voice.

'Great! That's the girl!' He watched thoughtfully as she spooned up the last of her treacle pudding. Her appetite might appear healthy enough, but he hadn't missed that note of defiance in her voice. He'd noticed the dark smudges around her eyes too and the wistful, slightly sad look that dimmed her usual sparkle. He had almost asked her how she had enjoyed the film last night—nearly admitted that he had been at the cinema himself and had spotted her as he had been on his way out. He'd seen Bobby Carr too, his arm around a tall sophisticated girl who had reminded him of Heather. At the time he hadn't been sure whether Dee had seen him too. Now he knew.

*   *   *

Bobby was leaning against the door of the flat when Dee got to the top of the stairs. He wore well-cut slacks and an expensive-looking blue cashmere sweater. The handsome features were arranged in their usual confident smile, exuding a bland innocence that was totally deceptive.

'Well, I thought you'd never show up!' He grasped her round the waist and drew her close. 'I've missed you. Don't I get a kiss?'

Dee could hardly believe that anyone could be so brash and deceitful. 'Why are you here, Bobby?' she asked, pushing him aside and fumbling in her pocket for her key.

'Well, that's a nice welcome, I must say!' He stared at her in outraged surprise, following her into the flat and standing by the door as she took off her cape and started washing the breakfast things that she and Claire had left soaking in the sink. After watching thoughtfully for a moment he came up behind and slid his arms around her. 'For God's sake, Dee, can't you leave that? I haven't seen you for days. I want to make up for lost time.'

She turned the full force of her blazing eyes on him. 'I thought you were doing that last night!' she told him icily. 'With Geraldine—at the cinema!'

The smile vanished from his face and he stared at her. 'You were there too?'

She nodded. 'Yes, I was there too, with your sister Angie, as a matter of fact. I got rather tired of waiting for you to ring, so when she asked me to join her for shopping and a film . . .' He was shaking his head impatiently.

'Look—it wasn't the way it looked, Dee.'

'Oh? Then how *was* it?'

'I called in on Ma yesterday afternoon. Gerry was there having tea and she was at a loose end. Ma

suggested that we teamed up and went to the film.'
He spread his hands. 'There was nothing in it.'

Dee turned away from him. His mother had en-
gineered the whole thing. She had even manipulated
Angie; kind, thoughtful Angie who'd die rather than
hurt anyone! But Bobby didn't *have* to go along with it,
did he?

He grasped her arm and turned her roughly towards
him. 'God! You didn't think . . . ?' He laughed in a way
that jarred on her raw nerves. 'You really are the end,
Dee! Anyway, I'm here now, so what are we going to
do?'

She stared at him. 'I see. You're here *now*, so that
makes it all right, does it?' She shook her head. 'Anyway, I can't go out with you this evening, I have something arranged.'

His eyes hardened. 'So cancel it!'

'I can't do that. When I make a promise I keep it.' Dee
turned back to the washing-up.

Bobby threw up his hands exasperatedly. 'What do
you mean anyway, you've got "something else
arranged"? It can't be *that* important, surely? I thought
we were supposed to be engaged.'

She spun round, her eyes bright. 'So did I! It didn't
seem to be stopping you, though—last night . . .'

He interrupted with a loud, explosive laugh. 'Oh, I
see! That's what all this is about, is it? Look, surely
you're not as petty-minded as that? I've said I'm sorry.
What do you want me to do—eat dirt?'

'I don't want you to do anything. I've told you, I
already have a date for tonight. And I intend to keep it.'
She turned back to the sink and continued with the
washing-up, but Bobby took her arm and pulled her
round to face him.

'*Don't turn away from me like that!*' His blue eyes
glinted like ice and his fingers were painfully hard on her

upper arms. 'Okay then, you can't make it tonight, but you will be at the race on Friday, won't you?'

She sighed. 'I told you, Bobby, I can't. It's impossible. I'll be on duty.'

He shook her. 'Look, Dee, this is important to me —to us. I've promised you that I'll give up racing if I win . . .'

'*If* you win?' She was staring at him.

His brows drew together angrily. 'All right, *when* I win! I think the least you could do is to be there! You seem to want *me* to be the one to make all the sacrifices, but there is a limit!' The eyes that stared into hers were almost menacing. 'Just don't overstep the mark, or I'm warning you . . .' The outer door slammed and the kitchen door burst open to reveal Claire.

'Hello, I've been—*Oh*! I'm sorry.' She stood in the doorway, looking at the two angry faces, acutely embarrassed. 'I—er—I'll just go and take off my coat.' She disappeared rapidly into her bedroom, closing the door firmly behind her, and Dee looked at Bobby challengingly.

'You were about to warn me . . .' she invited.

He stared at her coldly. 'All right, have it your way. Go out on your date—if you really *do* have one! And stay away from the race just like you always do. I'm not giving you the chance to change your mind, Dee, because you don't deserve it. When you're ready to apologise you know where I am!' And with that he turned and walked out of the flat, slamming the door behind him.

CHAPTER FIVE

THE door of the ground floor flat was ajar, and Dee let herself in. The living room floor space was crowded with half unpacked tea chests, the furniture strewn with clothes, curtains and books; but a delicious spicy aroma drifted through from the direction of the kitchen and Dee sniffed appreciatively as she stood looking round her. 'What are you making?' she called. 'It certainly smells professional!'

Greig popped his head round the door. He had changed into jeans and trainers, topped by one of his favourite sweat-shirts, and he grinned at her as he came into the room. 'Something I discovered in the super-market a few weeks ago. You just chuck everything in, then mix up this stuff from a packet, plus a dash of wine. It's fantastic—instant gourmet! And the beauty of it is, you can get on with something else while it cooks.'

She looked around her, raising one eyebrow at the muddle. 'Well, if this lot is anything to go by you won't be short of something to occupy the waiting time!'

He followed her gaze. 'This is the part I hate about moving. I usually try to ignore it all in the hope that it'll just go away.'

Dee began to pick up the books and stack them. 'Don't be such a slob!' She turned to him, a suspicious look in her eyes. 'Wait a minute—you didn't ask me down here this evening to . . . ?'

'No! I told you. I don't really mind if it stays like this,' he assured her. He paused, looking at her. 'By the way, I believe I passed your fiancé on my way in earlier.

He didn't look best pleased with life. I hope you haven't . . .'

'You needn't concern yourself with him,' she interrupted. 'Anyway, how did you know it was him?'

'Saw his photograph on your mantelpiece,' he explained. He glanced at her hesitantly. 'As a matter of fact I—er—saw him at the cinema last night. I saw you too. I gathered that you weren't together.'

She picked up a pair of curtains lying over the back of the settee and shook them vigorously. That was all she needed to add to her humiliation. 'These need ironing,' she said brusquely. 'Where are you going to hang them?'

Greig lifted his shoulders. 'In here, I thought. So you don't want to talk about it?'

She shook her head. 'Why should I? Anyway, there's nothing to talk about. If you can find the iron in all this mess I'll run these over for you.'

'Thanks. I *think* it's in that box over there.' He dipped into the box and came up with the iron. As he unwound the flex he glanced at her out of the corner of his eye. 'I—take it you knew he was seeing someone else, then?'

Dee rounded on him, her eyes flashing. 'Mind your own damned business!' She snatched the iron from him. 'And if you want me to iron these curtains you'll have to find the ironing board too!'

He took a deep breath and dusted off his hands. 'Right—yes. I'll get it.'

After unfolding the board for her he retreated to the kitchen to put the finishing touches to the meal. From the living room he could hear her putting a great deal of energy into ironing his curtains, banging the iron down with more force than was strictly necessary as she worked. When he put his head round the door ten minutes later to tell her the meal was ready he found her standing on a chair, struggling to hang the curtains at the large bay window.

'Grub up! Hey, why didn't you ask me to help with that?' Gently but firmly he helped her down from the chair she was standing on and made short work of hanging the curtains himself. 'There,' he said, standing back to admire them. 'The place is looking more like home already.' He turned to grin at her. 'What's that they say about a "woman's touch"?'

Dee flicked a piece of cotton from the wine-red fabric. 'They do look nice, don't they? They're very good material. Did they come from your last flat?'

He nodded. 'That's right. The last relic from the marital home; used to hang in my study.' He gave her a slightly sheepish grin. 'I got custody of them.'

Suddenly she felt ashamed of herself. 'Oh—I'm sorry. Look, I shouldn't have blown my top like that. It was just . . .'

'That I touched you on the raw.' Greig reached out to rest his hands lightly on her shoulders, smiling gently down at her. 'It's I who should be apologising. I got what I asked for. It's just that I hate to see you rushing headlong down the same path as I did. I can't just stand by and watch without doing—saying *something*.' He smiled and the hazel eyes suddenly twinkled warmly at her. 'Come on—dinner's spoiling.'

Greig's 'instant gourmet' turned out to be a spicy chicken casserole and, as he had assured her, it was very good. To follow he had bought fruit and cheese and a very passable white wine with which to wash it all down. Dee was quick to congratulate him.

'If it was me who'd just moved in I'd be eating sandwiches or egg on toast. That was very nice.' She looked around. 'Now, what can I do in return?'

He shook his head, getting up from the table to plug in the coffee-maker. 'Wouldn't dream of it! You've already done the curtains for me. I really didn't ask you down here to work, in spite of what you think.'

Dee sat back in her chair, watching him setting out coffee cups and saucers. 'You were right about the cinema. Bobby was there with someone else,' she volunteered at last. 'And we did have a row over it. It's just another of the things we don't seem able to agree on. Bobby can't see why I mind if he goes out with other girls.' She looked up at him appealingly. 'Is it so unreasonable to expect him to be faithful to me?'

Greig resumed his seat opposite her, looking back into the enormous green eyes. She quite obviously had no idea of the effect those eyes had on him. What the hell was wrong with Bobby Carr anyway? he asked himself angrily. Couldn't he see when he was on to a good thing? But he'd already said more than he'd intended. He shrugged noncommittally. 'Of course it isn't.'

She looked at him intently. 'Greig, what did you mean earlier—when you said I was rushing headlong down the same path as you?'

He hesitated for so long before speaking that for a moment she thought he hadn't heard what she said; then he looked up. When his eyes met hers they were clouded with something she couldn't read. 'Your Bobby has a giant ego,' he said quietly. 'It doesn't take a genius to see that. Anyway, it's something I happen to be an expert on. I married someone like that myself, you see, and I had as much trouble handling it as you seem to be having.' He paused, wondering just how much he should say to her, then decided to take a chance. After all, what was the point of a painful experience if you didn't use it to help others? 'That kind of ego is cannibalistic,' he went on. 'It's voracious. It feeds on everything and *everyone* round it, swallows you up till there's nothing left. If you let it, it uses up all your resources, saps every ounce of your energy and drains the emotions dry.' The golden eyes were grave as they met hers. 'You have to love that person with total selflessness, with every shred

of your being, to be able to live with that. You have to be the kind of person who wants nothing for yourself—to be prepared for your own personality to be completely submerged.' He reached for the coffee-pot. 'I wasn't that unselfish and—for what it's worth—I don't think you are either, Dee. You have your own dreams and ambitions, and from what I've seen they don't include pandering to . . .' He bit back the rest of the sentence, shaking his head. 'I'd better leave it there. I think I've said enough.'

The silence hung heavily between them as he poured coffee into the cups. Dee took a sip, then looked up at him and said quietly: 'The irony of it is that I didn't even want to go out with him at first. He was a patient, here at Queen Eleanor's. He broke his leg in an accident. He just kept on and on after he was discharged—flowers, chocolates, telephone calls. I didn't even *like* him, but in the end . . .'

'He wore you down,' Greig completed. 'You were another challenge. If you'd agreed to go out with him right away there would have been two dates – maybe three, and then . . .' He clicked his fingers. 'Over!'

She sighed. 'As it is—it's too late.'

'You mean you're in love with him—deeply in love?' His eyes searched hers.

Dee was silent. For a long time now she'd been having serious doubts about the nature of her feelings towards Bobby. Was what they felt for each other love in the true sense of the word? He *wanted* her, that much was for sure. And she had dreamed of being married to him —setting up home and sharing a life with him. He could be such fun—so charming and attentive—when he was in a good mood. Lately though, she had seen another side of him; a less attractive side. But no one was perfect, she had argued with herself; Bobby was under a lot of pressure. Once he had given up racing and settled down

in his father's firm . . . But if that wasn't what he wanted—if she was pushing him against his will as Claire had hinted—what then? Suddenly she thought of her father. There was a time when she could have gone to him with this; when he would have listened sympathetically and given her good, wise advice. Tears filled her eyes. It seemed there was no one now in whom she could confide.

Without speaking Greig covered her hand with his. 'Look—I'm sorry. I've upset you—said too much. Who am I to unsettle you? After all, we hardly know each other.'

She shook her head. 'In a way that makes it easier. I'm grateful, Greig. I know there's a lot of truth in what you've said. You've helped to crystallise my own thoughts. But it isn't quite like you've been saying.' She looked up into his eyes. 'Bobby has promised to give up his racing if I'll marry him. He knows how much I hate it and he's willing . . .'

'*Is* he?' The look in his eyes stopped her from completing her sentence. That look, and those two brief words, carried all the doubts she had felt herself—echoed everything that Claire had tried to say, but the solution still eluded her.

She sighed deeply. 'If only I knew the answer to it all! I know all the pitfalls and it's easy for others to warn, but . . .'

The hand that covered hers pressed warmly. 'Look, Dee—when all's said and done there's only one thing that counts above all others,' he told her gently. 'If you love him—*really* love him, you can forget the rest. Somehow you'll ride it all out.'

'Forgive me for asking, but didn't you believe that yourself?' she asked, meeting his eyes with the frank, direct gaze that he found so disarming.

He couldn't quite meet it as he said: 'Ah, that's

another story. I wouldn't want to sour your illusions with it. In my case I was bowled over—hopelessly flattered.' He gave her a bitter little smile. 'It's something we poor males are rather prone to, I'm afraid.' He grinned at her wryly. 'You know what they say—"The bigger they are, the harder they fall!"'

Suddenly she felt a rush of warmth towards him and her fingers curled around his and squeezed gently. 'Thanks for telling me about it,' she said softly. 'It can't have been easy. But you mustn't worry about me. I'll be fine.' She smiled into his eyes as she glanced at her watch and rose to her feet. 'And now I think I'd better go, don't you?'

He walked with her to the door. 'Thanks for helping me hang the curtains.'

She turned to look up at him. 'And thank *you* for trying to help me sort out my problems.' She laughed. '*And* for the meal. It was delicious!'

He looked at her, smiling up at him with those huge green eyes, her lips slightly parted. She looked so young, so heartachingly defenceless that he found himself suddenly wanting to wrap his arms around her and hold her close and safe where no one could hurt her again. With an effort he pulled himself together. He was getting soft and sentimental. It must be the onset of middle age! But he did allow himself to lean forward and brush his lips across her cheek.

'Any time you want a shoulder to cry on—or another "instant gourmet" meal,' he told lightly, 'you know where I live.' He gave a helpless shrug, looking round the littered room. 'And who knows—maybe next time it'll even look civilised!'

Dee walked up the three flights to the Bird's Nest very slowly. She had never met anyone like Greig Meredith before. He seemed worldly-wise, yet he wasn't cynical.

He'd obviously been badly hurt, yet he wasn't bitter. It must have cost him quite a lot to talk to her as he had this evening. Opening old wounds was always painful. He had done it out of genuine concern, yet he hardly knew her. Unbidden came the sudden memory of the warm, comforting pressure of his hand on hers—of his lips briefly caressing her cheek. By the time she had reached the top floor she had decided that Greig Meredith was a very remarkable man.

As she opened the door of the flat she could hear Claire speaking on the telephone in the kitchen:

'No, I haven't a clue what time she'll be home—oh, wait a minute, I think that's her now.' She pushed open the door, gesturing and silently mouthing at Dee: 'It's Bobby—will you speak to him?' Dee indicated that she would, and Claire returned to the phone. 'Yes, it is her. Hang on a minute.' She handed the receiver over and made herself scarce.

Dee took a deep breath and said: 'Hello, Bobby.'

'So you got home, then?' He sounded subdued.

'Yes, I got home.'

'Have a good time?'

'Yes, thank you.'

There was a small silence, then he said: 'Look, Dee, I'm no good at apologies, you know that, but I just wanted to say that I shouldn't have lost my rag with you.'

'It's all right.'

'No, it isn't. I'm sorry about the cinema too. I should have rung you first. You'd been saying you wanted to see that film.'

So he hadn't rung her, then? 'I think we'd both better forget it, Bobby,' she said quietly. 'I'm sorry too—that I can't be at the race on Friday. But this isn't like any other job, you know. Anyway, if I'm honest I hate to see you risking your life.'

'I know.' There was a pause, then he asked: 'Can I

come round and collect you now? We could have a drink, there's this little club I know.'

'It's late, Bobby.' Dee looked at her watch. It was after eleven. 'I'd like to, really, but I have to be on duty at eight in the morning.'

'If you really wanted to see me you'd say yes,' he said, his voice sulky at the other end of the line.

Dee bit her lip. Why would he never try to understand? 'Of course I want to see you, Bobby,' she said patiently. 'It's just . . .'

'You wouldn't even put this other date off for me. Who *did* you go out with, anyway?' There was an imperious note to his voice now and she sighed.

'I was invited downstairs to the ground floor flat for dinner, that's all.' She was getting as devious as him, she chided herself.

'I shan't see you till after the race, then,' he said.

'I'm free tomorrow evening,' she told him.

'Too much to do. Tonight was the last chance,' he said stubbornly. 'Well, good night then, Dee. I'll pick you up around eight on Friday evening, for the party.'

'All right. Good night, Bobby—and good luck for the race.' After she had replaced the receiver she stood for a long time, just staring at the instrument on the wall. Was she being unfair? She really *should* be there to lend him her support on Friday, however much she hated it. Maybe she was asking too much of him in expecting him to give up racing for her. Maybe they were asking too much of each other. Perhaps on Friday she would tell him she wouldn't hold him to his promise. But somehow the thought only depressed her more than ever.

'So this "maintenance man" who gave you a lift out to the track actually turned out to be the new orthopaedic consultant all the time? What a hoot!' Claire rocked with laughter. 'You must have had a shock when you came face to face with him in the theatre this morning; especially when you'd spent most of Saturday kindly allowing him to paint our kitchen! I can't get over it!'

The two girls were having a last cup of coffee together and catching up on the weekend's happenings.

'You have to admit he's not the usual consultant type,' Dee pointed out. 'Naturally, I was furious at first. I thought it was a dirty trick, his letting me believe he was on the maintenance staff. But after this evening I've really come to the conclusion that he prefers to be thought of in those terms. He actually described his work as "people maintenance".'

Claire smiled. 'I'm getting to like the sound of him. And he cooked you a meal—his first night in his new flat. You must have made quite a hit!'

'An "olive branch", he called it. To make up for the deception.' Dee looked up at her friend, suddenly deciding to confide in her. 'Claire—when Angie and I were at the cinema last night I saw Bobby. He was with another girl.'

The smile left Claire's face. 'I knew something was wrong the moment you walked in last night. It must have been awkward for Angie. What did she say?'

Dee shook her head. 'She didn't see—she was looking for a lost glove at the time. I didn't tell her.'

'So *that* was what you and Bobby were arguing about earlier. I suppose he rang to apologise.'

'He apologised for going out without me, but not for taking out another girl,' Dee told her. 'And then he was annoyed because I wouldn't let him come round tonight.' She sighed. 'The fact that I won't be at the race on Friday hardly helped either. So now things are as bad as ever.'

Claire opened her mouth and then closed it again, not

sure how what she had to say would be received. But Dee knew her friend too well to miss what was going through her mind.

'You think the whole thing's a disaster,' she said for her. 'That seems to be the general consensus of opinion. You think I should end the relationship, don't you?' she asked.

Claire sighed. 'I have to admit I think it would be for the best, love. You're so totally unsuited to each other. I know it will hurt, but it might be better to make a clean break.'

Dee was silent for a long moment, then she said almost in a whisper: 'I couldn't do it before the race. And we're supposed to be announcing our engagement at the party afterwards.'

Claire nodded sympathetically. 'I know. It's never easy, and in this case I can see it's going to be doubly difficult.' She uncurled her long legs and stood up, looking down at Dee. 'Why not sleep on it? Things always look better in the clear light of day.'

Things were busy in Theatre One next morning. After the recent warming up of the weather there had been an early morning fog, resulting in a bad pile-up on the motorway. For most of the morning shift they were dealing with the victims. Most of the operations carried out were emergency repair work on fractures and to stop internal bleeding. Many of the patients would need further surgery later, when swelling and bleeding had reduced and they could be diagnosed in more detail. Dee's work as scrub-nurse was concentrated and intense and by the end of the shift she was exhausted. She was barely listening to Nurse Hastings' chatter as they changed out of their theatre gear, but suddenly a phrase caught her attention:

'. . . Brighton bombing. It was in all the papers at the

time. Now the *Echo* seems to have got hold of it. And I heard a rumour that one of his patients was a famous politician.'

'What was that?' Dee turned to look at the young second-year nurse.

'Mr Meredith—you know, the new orthopaedic consultant. He worked on some of the victims of the Brighton bombing—seems to have been quite a hero at the time. There's a piece about him in the *Echo* today. Have you seen it?'

Dee shook her head. 'No. I haven't had a chance to look at the paper yet. I wonder how they got hold of the story?'

Sister Fairchild chimed in: 'There's always a mole on every hospital's staff, if you ask me,' she said darkly. 'Anything newsworthy seems to find its way to the local newspaper office as if by magic.'

Dee didn't give the matter another thought as she made her way to the senior nurses' rest room. Her mind was too busy with her own problem. She had decided to give the canteen a miss—have a snack lunch quietly in the rest room and try to work out what to do about Bobby. She was relieved to find the room empty and she settled down with her sandwiches, first filling and plugging in the coffee-maker.

After she had eaten she took a pad and pen from her bag and began to compose a letter. She had always found it helped to untangle her thoughts if she wrote them down on paper. After three attempts she thought she had crystallised her thoughts as kindly and as lucidly as she could. She addressed an envelope to Bobby, slipped the final letter inside and sealed it. If the worst came to the worst and she couldn't summon up the courage to tell him face to face she could always post the letter. It was a despicably cowardly thought and she knew that as long as the letter was there in her handbag she would some-

how find the strength to do what she had to without resorting to it.

When she had finished she looked at her watch and was surprised to find that it was almost four o'clock. Better get out to the shops before they closed and buy something for dinner!

Gathering up her things, she slipped on her cape and made for the door, but it flew open just as she was reaching for the handle and she almost collided with Sister Fairchild as she hurried in. In the confusion Dee dropped her bag, spilling some of its contents on to the floor, and Sister bent to help her pick up the scattered belongings, apologising profusely:

'I'm sorry, Staff. After this morning I'm all thumbs. Hectic, wasn't it?' Dee agreed that it was and Sister lowered her voice confidentially as she went on: 'As a matter of fact, Douglas – Mr Thurman has just asked if he can take me out to dinner this evening. It's such short notice and I'm hurrying home to wash my hair.'

'Oh—how lovely. I hope you have a nice time.' As Dee walked away down the corridor she couldn't help smiling. So Sister had managed to get Mr Thurman to take her out at last! No wonder she was in such a tizz! She took the lift down to the floor below and decided to stop off at Intensive Care to look in on one of the accident victims they had operated on that morning; a small boy with severe head injuries. The child had looked so tiny and fragile lying on the operating table that he had touched her heart-strings, and she couldn't go home without knowing how he was doing. Claire was able to assure her that he was holding his own and fighting back strongly. She even allowed Dee a peep into the curtained-off cubicle where the child lay peacefully sedated. He was breathing with the aid of a ventilator, surrounded by monitoring equipment.

'The parents are staying the night,' Claire told her

quietly. 'So far so good, but let's hope that when the oedema reduces there'll be no brain damage.' Dee nodded, reassured by the knowledge that everything possible had been done for the tiny patient; that he'd had—and was receiving—the best possible care.

On her way back to the lift Dee had to pass the office of the hospital administrator, Mr Jameson. She was just passing his door when it suddenly burst open and a tall, broad figure brandishing a folded newspaper burst through it like a hurricane. He slammed the door hard and turned abruptly, almost knocking Dee off her feet. She looked up in surprise as she recognised Greig, but before she could open her mouth to speak to him he had rushed past her unseeingly, his hazel eyes dark with fury and his unfastened white coat flying open. As he went he tore the newspaper in half in an angry gesture and stuffed it forcibly into a litter bin that stood in the corridor.

Dee stared after him. What on earth had got into him? He didn't even seem to have noticed her in spite of the fact that he'd almost knocked her over! Something must have happened to upset him. And she had a pretty fair idea what that might be.

CHAPTER SIX

As Dee opened the front door of Wedgwood House the sound of several voices all speaking at once assailed her ears. Half a dozen people stood in the hall, and she soon saw that they were crowded round Greig Meredith's door. A few of them wore cameras slung round their shoulders which, along with their obvious persistence, told her that they were probably reporters from various newspapers. Suddenly she heard Greig's unmistakable voice rise above the others:

'Get out, all of you! I've *told* you—you've got the wrong man. If you don't leave immediately I'm going to call the police! This is a hospital residence, not a bear-garden! There are people in this building trying to sleep!'

Dee could hear the note of desperation in his voice and she began to elbow her way through the crush of jostling journalists. 'Why are you bothering poor Wally like this?' she asked one of them innocently. 'Has he done something awful?'

A sudden silence fell as they all turned to look at her, and Greig seized on the opportunity to slam his door shut.

'*Wally*—Wally who?' one of the reporters asked, turning to look at her.

'Wally Smith. He's a maintenance man.' Dee turned wide green eyes on the man who had asked the question.

'He really *isn't* a surgeon, then—the one who had all the publicity over the Brighton bombing?'

Dee laughed. 'What, Wally? Does he *look* like a surgeon? Anyway, he wouldn't be living here if he was, would he?' She turned to look at the name panel next to

73

the doorbell, hoping that Greig's name wasn't on it. To her relief he hadn't got round to inserting it yet. 'Oh look, he's closed his door,' she said in surprise. 'I'm afraid that must be my fault. Shall I get him to open it again for you? He's quite nice-looking and I believe he has a black belt in judo. I'm sure you'd like a picture of him for your paper.' She raised her hand to knock, but the reporters were already moving away, muttering moodily to each other. She waited till she was quite sure they had gone, then tapped softly on Greig's door. 'It's all right, you can come out now,' she called through the keyhole.

He opened the door and peered round it, grinning at her slightly shamefacedly. He was dressed in his favourite off-duty wear of jeans and sweatshirt. 'Thanks for getting rid of them. You'd better come in before they discover all that was a bunch of lies and come back!'

Inside he closed the door and looked at her, a half-smile on his lips. 'I must congratulate you on your quick thinking. Can't say I think much of the alias you picked for me, though.'

Dee laughed. '"Wally" was the first name that sprang to mind.' She raised an insolent eyebrow at him. 'Do you think there's a subconscious message there?'

'Very definitely! But thanks again, anyway. Want a coffee? I've just brewed some.' He began to walk towards the kitchen, taking her affirmative for granted.

She looked around the room. In spite of what he had said about his habitual untidiness, it now looked quite neat and homelike—books in the bookcase, furniture tastefully rearranged and all the chaotic clutter of the previous evening gone. 'You've done a good job in here!' she called out to him. 'It looks very nice.'

'All in the hope that you'd come visiting again,' he told her as he came back into the room with two mugs of coffee on a tray. 'You should see the rest of the flat!'

She looked at him enquiringly. 'Well, are you going to explain to me what all that out there was about?'

Greig put the tray down on the table and ran a hand through his already rumpled hair. 'Oh lord, do I really have to?'

'Yes, I think you do, seeing that you have me to thank for your deliverance.' She took the mug he handed her. 'I did hear that there was a piece about your work with the victims of the Brighton bombing in the local paper, though I haven't had time to read it yet—and although you didn't see me, I witnessed your angry retreat from Mr Jameson's office this afternoon.'

He spread his hands. 'So what more do you need to know? That says it all.'

Dee shook her head. 'No, it doesn't. I want the inside story. What really happened? Is it true, and if it is, why are you so reluctant for people to know about it?'

Greig sighed deeply, sitting down on the arm of the settee. 'I just did my job, that was all. Look, if it had been Joe Bloggs from down the road, injured in a street accident, no one would have given what I did another thought.' He took a long drink of his coffee. 'I hate this thing of only violent or dramatic happenings being news. There are hundreds of accidents every week and a hundred other surgeons are doing what I did all the time.' He looked at her for a moment, then said: 'My father was badly injured in a colliery accident twelve years ago. It cost him the use of his legs. No one made a song and dance out of that!'

Dee began to see his point. She shrugged. 'So why don't you tell them that? It makes your point strongly.'

'I don't want to *make any points*! I don't want any publicity at all!' he almost shouted at her. 'Look, I chose to come and work at this hospital because of the high accident rate on the motorway nearby. I thought my particular skills would be useful here. Why can't anyone

understand that and leave me alone to get on with it?'

She smiled. 'Do you know that when you're angry your Welsh accent gets stronger and stronger?'

'*So?* Anything wrong with that?' His chin thrust out challengingly at her, the hazel eyes darkening, and Dee had to bite the inside of her lip hard to stop herself from laughing.

'Of course not,' she said gently. 'It wasn't meant as a criticism. I think it sounds very attractive, if you want to know.'

He checked, searching her eyes, then suddenly his expression softened and he began to smile. 'Are you taking the mickey, Nurse Latimer?'

With great relief Dee allowed the grin full rein. 'Only ever so slightly, I promise,' she admitted.

He sighed, relaxing visibly. 'I'm sorry if I went over the top. It's just that it gets my goat. I don't seem to have had a moment's peace since the night of the tragedy. I thought when I came here it'd be over, but now it looks as though it's followed me yet again. That's why you saw me coming out of the HA's office this afternoon. But even he couldn't throw any light on where the story came from. I just can't *stand* people staring at me—talking about me as though I'd done something special.'

'Was that why you let me go on thinking you were a maintenance man the other day?' she asked.

Greig nodded, his lips twitching with amusement. 'It was so refreshing. I really enjoyed it.' He gave her a wry grin. 'I even enjoyed your haughty, patronising attitude.'

'Only because you were looking forward to getting your own back!' she countered crisply.

He laughed. 'Well, you could be right there, I suppose!'

Dee swallowed the last of her coffee and stood up. 'Well, this won't do. I'm supposed to be cooking the evening meal and I haven't done a thing towards it yet.'

He walked to the door with her. 'Busy this evening?'

She turned to look up at him. 'Not particularly—why?'

He lifted his shoulders. 'I'd like to give you dinner —as a thank-you for saving me from those vultures.' He raised an eyebrow at her. 'What do you say?'

Dee smiled. 'Instant gourmet again?'

Greig shook his head. 'I thought maybe a restaurant this time. I might even allow you the pleasure of seeing me in a suit for the first time!'

Dee hesitated. It had been a tiring, traumatic day. Bobby had made it clear that he would be busy until after the race—and anyway, she was ending her relationship with Bobby. A chill came over her at the thought of the hours spent composing the letter in her handbag and the scene she had yet to face. She didn't want to think about it any more—not today.

'If you have something else on—or if you think that Bobby . . .'

'No, it isn't that. I'd love to—honestly,' she told him quickly.

He looked down at her, frowning a little as he searched her clouded eyes. 'You're *sure*?'

'I'm sure.'

'Right. I'll pick you up at about eight.'

Although the restaurant was elegant and expensive and the meal was delicious, Dee seemed subdued. Greig was concerned. He wondered if she had come out with him simply to be polite. Or, worse, to get her own back on Bobby Carr. Neither idea appealed to him very much. Examining his feelings, he decided that he was conceited enough to want her to have accepted his invitation because she liked his company. She was looking especially lovely this evening with the bright, silky hair loose about her shoulders—wearing a dress of a deep, vibrant blue that made her skin look almost translucent and softened the green of those almond-shaped eyes to turquoise. As they were drinking their coffee he decided to ask her outright about her mood.

'What is it, Dee—sorry you came?'

She looked up, startled. 'What? No, of course not. What makes you ask?'

He shrugged. 'You're unusually quiet. Forgive me, but it crossed my mind that you might be using this evening to get back at that fiancé of yours and maybe you were regretting it.' He shook his head. 'Not that I'm complaining, mind. You're here—that's all that really matters.'

Dee bit her lip. 'I'm sorry. Have I really been that bad?' She stirred her coffee thoughtfully. 'Bobby never actually was my fiancé, you know,' she told him. 'Not officially, anyway—and now—now he never will be.'

'Ah, I knew there was something.' Greig regarded her for a moment. 'Want to talk about it?'

She paused momentarily before her eyes met his. 'I'd like to tell someone, yes.'

He beckoned the waiter. 'Just let me pay the bill and we'll go somewhere quiet.'

He said no more until they were outside and in the car, then he turned to her. 'Do you want to go back to the flat or on somewhere for a quiet drink?'

'You don't have to entertain me,' she told him. 'There really isn't much to say about it. I've decided to finish with Bobby. After the race on Friday I'm going to tell him it's all off.'

'I see.' He looked at her. 'I hope it isn't because of anything I've said.'

She shook her head. 'Claire's been voicing opinions on the subject too. You weren't the only one. But I had my own doubts anyway—grave doubts.'

Greig lifted his shoulders helplessly. 'What can I say? Look, Dee, if there's anything I can do to help . . . How

do you feel about it?'

She sighed. 'I just wish it was all over and behind me. I'd like to make the break right away and get it over with, but it wouldn't be fair to put any more pressure on him until after Friday.'

'You're sure it's what you want?' he asked. 'You've done nothing irrevocable, you know. You could always change your mind.'

'I shan't. I know it's right,' she told him. 'I believe I've known for a long time. I just lacked the courage to end it—I still do.'

They were both silent for a moment, then he asked her: 'Do you want to go home?'

She shrugged. 'I suppose so.'

She sounded so despondent that his heart twisted within him. 'I'll make you some coffee,' he offered. 'And we'll listen to some records. We needn't talk at all if you don't feel like it.'

Dee turned to smile at him. 'You understand, don't you? You've been through all this too.'

He felt for her hand and squeezed it. 'Let's just say there's no fool like an old fool,' he said enigmatically.

He was as good as his word. They drank coffee and listened to the most soothing records Greig could find among his collection. They spoke the minimum of words, each busy with their own thoughts.

Dee seemed to relax in the quiet peaceful atmosphere, but Greig was far from relaxed as he watched her unwind. Each time he saw her—talked to her, it grew worse: this feeling of wanting to protect her. He wasn't fool enough to believe the fatuous excuses he made to himself—that it was the frustrated father in him coming out—that he'd have felt the same towards any young girl who'd been badly treated. Might as well admit that there was nothing noble about the way he felt. He was attracted to her, damn it! Plain old *physically* attracted, and there was an end of it! Being close to her as he was at this moment was becoming torture. Like any other red-blooded male he wanted to touch her—kiss her—wanted to feel her arms around him, her fingers in his hair, her lips flowering beneath his. He drew in his breath sharply. Good *God*, he really must get a hold on himself!

Dee glanced at him out of the corner of her eye. Had he just yawned? She looked surreptitiously at her watch. She mustn't outstay her welcome. He'd been kind to her—more than kind. He wanted to repay her for helping to get rid of those reporters this afternoon, but she mustn't presume too much on his good nature. She made a small exclamation about the time and got to her feet.

'Heavens, I'd no idea it was so late! I'd better go and let you get to bed.' He was standing too and she turned to him. 'Thank you for this evening, Greig. I really did enjoy the meal. I'm afraid I wasn't very good company, though. I hope I haven't been too boring.'

Greig looked down into the sea-green eyes. Boring! If she only knew! 'Not at all,' he told her. 'And you don't have to rush off, you know. Perhaps you'd like a brandy —or another coffee?' His cool tone betrayed nothing of the longing he felt to keep her here just a little longer. He was imagining how the place would feel when she'd gone—empty—nothing left but a tantalising whiff of her perfume to remind him . . .

She shook her head. 'I mustn't—but thanks.' Suddenly she reached up and put her hands on his shoulders. 'Thanks again, Greig—for the meal and the talk and everything.' She stood on tiptoe and her lips brushed his cheek. 'It really helped.'

It was just too much. Like a reflex action his arms closed round her and his lips found hers. His kiss was tender; with a massive effort he held back the hunger that had been slowly building inside him all evening.

This wasn't the right time to be kissing her, he knew that.
And he wouldn't have if—if she hadn't . . . To his
surprise he felt her lips respond beneath his, amazingly it
was almost as though she had wanted him to kiss her. He
paused, raising his head to look briefly into her eyes,
then, his arms drawing her closer, he kissed her again,
this time unleashing some of the passion welling up
within him. When at last he reluctantly released her they
were both trembling.

She looked up at him, her cheeks flushed and the
green eyes bright as emeralds. Shaking her head a little,
she said: 'I'd—er—better be going.'

His eyes raked her face for the smallest sign of regret
—embarrassment. 'Yes, I suppose so.' His arms dropped
to his side. He felt tongue-tied. He longed to know her
true reaction. Her face revealed nothing. Had her response been sheer impulse—she was especially vulnerable just now—on the rebound? Perhaps she was angry—
with him—with herself? He opened his mouth to say
something—*anything*. He'd no idea what, but . . .

'Good night, Greig.'

She was gone, and he was left standing there, shaken
to the core by the certain knowledge that for the first
time—the *very* first time in his thirty-six years, he was in
love. Yes, actually in love!

Claire was out, and Dee was grateful to have the flat to
herself for once. She knew she could not have fooled
Claire into believing that nothing had happened. Even
looking at her own face in the mirror she could see it; the
two bright spots of colour burning in her cheeks, the
unusual brilliance of her eyes. She looked almost as
though she had a fever. Claire would have asked questions she couldn't answer because she didn't yet know
the answers herself.

She undressed quickly and got into bed. Lying there in

the dark she tried to collect her thoughts. Greig had made a special effort this evening. He had looked so handsome in what he laughingly told her was his only suit; his 'establishment set'; kept only for interviews and special occasions. Dark grey and very sober, teamed with a gleaming white shirt and striped tie, it made him look distinguished and highly respectable. He had been so kind and understanding—made no demands on her. And she had felt so relaxed, so comfortable.

When she had reached out to touch him—to kiss his cheek she had done it out of friendship; gratitude for his help and understanding. At least, she *thought* she had. But then everything had changed. When he had kissed her something magical had happened. Never before had she felt like that. It was as though some other force had taken her over, sparked off an explosion of stars inside her that set all her senses tingling. For a few breathless moments she had been lifted out of herself—lifted to heights she had never known existed. What did it mean? She turned over and curled into a ball, not even trying to blot out the image of Greig's face that seemed imprinted on the insides of her eyelids; making no attempt at all to shrug off the warmth of his arms, still lingering, or the tender pressure of his lips on hers. For the first time in months Bobby occupied no corner of her mind at all.

Three floors below in the ground floor flat Greig lay wide awake too. Staring at the ceiling in the darkened bedroom, he asked himself what on earth he had done. His timing couldn't have been worse! If he'd wanted Dee why couldn't he have waited till she was over her broken engagement—till he could be sure that what she was feeling wasn't merely reaction? He punched his pillow viciously. Anyway, what was he thinking of—a man of his age? Who was he kidding? The girl was young enough to be—well, no, not quite his daughter, but anyway too young. He chewed his lip hard, trying not to remember the softness of her hair brushing his cheek, the delicious scent of her; the slender strength of her body against his. *Damn!* Coming here was turning out to be yet another bad mistake. His life was littered with them! Closing his eyes, he saw again the hated newspaper headlines that had dogged him for the past two years: BRILLIANT SURGEON SAVES MP FROM LIFE IN WHEELCHAIR. He sighed. Brilliant surgeon?—Idiot man!

Bobby felt good. It was his big day. The day he had waited for—looked forward to for months. No one was going to stop him now. No one was going to spoil it for him. He was here to win!

As he strapped on his helmet he glanced around. The track was crowded, the stands full of spectators. The air danced with a haze made of heat and petrol fumes; its pungent odour filled his nostrils and started the adrenalin coursing through his veins. The national papers as well as the local ones had already interviewed him and taken photographs, and the race was being covered by TV and radio teams. His bike was ready and his crew was waiting in the pits. Sitting astride the V4, he revved, grinning with satisfaction as he felt the great machine leap and roar with contained power beneath him, just waiting to be unleashed like a great, snarling wild animal. He rode up to take up his position on the front row of the grid. He'd practised hard—been over and over the track till he knew every bump and kink on it. Nothing could go wrong. Nothing could stop him now. He couldn't wait for the flag. This was going to be *his* day. He could feel it in the warmth of the sun of his face, the wind in his ears; the exciting vibration of the machine beneath him and in every tingling nerve of his body.

The race was in full spate when it happened. Bobby

was among the first half dozen racers as they took a sharp bend. In the outside line the bike in front of him suddenly seemed to go out of control. It skidded, the rider parted company with it and the bike slid crazily across the track in his path. There was no way he could avoid it. It was all over in a flash. To the horror of the helpless spectators two loud explosions rent the air as the petrol tanks burst. A pall of black smoke rose, obscuring the devastation on the track as more bikes sped helplessly into the debris. But even as the smoke began to clear help was arriving on the scene. The first-aid and ambulance crews found four injured men —miraculously, three had only superficial injuries, but the third, the man strongly tipped to win the Grand Prix, was in a bad way.

It was near the end of the late shift at Queen Eleanor's Accident and Emergency Department when word came in of the Grand Prix crash. The victims began to arrive ten minutes later; three were attended to by the Casualty Officer and later sent up to the ward to be admitted. The fourth lay unconscious and intubated in a cubicle. Mr Thurman arrived as a staff nurse was cutting away what was left of the racing leathers. He shook his head as the damaged legs were revealed and he saw the injuries the man had suffered.

'It could be a case for amputation,' he said, shaking his head as he looked at the shattered limbs. 'Better get Mr Meredith down immediately to have a look.' He began further examination as the nurse went off to telephone. 'Lucky for him those leathers were so well padded,' he muttered to himself. 'At least most of the skin is still intact.' The surgeon checked the young man's pulse and respiration, nodding to himself. 'Responding well to emergency treatment,' he muttered. 'Youth on his side—so far, so good.'

Theatre One had been alerted to expect an emergency accident case. As usual it would be repair work, to alleviate the risk of complications and arrest bleeding. Dee prepared the trolley as the patient was being anaesthetised. Mr Thurman and Greig were scrubbing up in the surgeons' room, examining the patient's X-rays which had been rushed up from Radiology. It seemed that the risk of amputation was less than Mr Thurman had at first suspected. There was a minimum of surface wounding, which meant less likelihood of bone infection. But the internal bone damage would be a major job, to be undertaken later, when shock had subsided and the patient's other injuries had had time to be properly assessed. As they entered the theatre Dee looked up and smiled at Greig over her mask, but his eyes looked unsmilingly back into hers with a troubled expression she didn't understand. But there was no time for words. The patient was wheeled into the theatre and transferred to the operating table. Dee took up her position, uncovering her trolley of instruments—then she glanced at the patient's face and all the blood seemed to drain from her, leaving her cold and shaken. Greig moved closer to her.

'I'm sorry, Dee,' he whispered. 'There was no way I could warn you. Shall I get Sister to take over?'

But she shook her head, breathing deeply to steady herself. '*No!* No, I'm—I'll be all right.' She looked down at Bobby's deathly pale face as he lay on the table. She could see that his injuries were terrible. The thing she had always dreaded had happened, just as she had imagined in her worst nightmares. She felt her head begin to reel and took another deep breath, urging her professionalism to take over as she obeyed the commands of the two surgeons. If she opted out now she knew would never forgive herself. At least she could do this for Bobby. It might be the last thing she ever did for him.

CHAPTER SEVEN

DEE sat by the bed in the curtained-off cubicle in Intensive Care. She had been sitting here ever since she came off duty an hour ago, watching Bobby's face for the slightest change, the merest flicker. The operation to stop the bleeding and assess the full extent of his injuries had drained her inner resources to the limit. Bobby had sustained several broken ribs, a broken collarbone and bruising to the kidneys, though luckily the internal injuries were not too serious. His sturdy racing helmet had kept head injury down to concussion only. At first it had been feared that his back was broken, but X-rays had shown that, although several vertebrae were seriously jarred, the spinal column was still mercifully intact. His legs, however, caused the greatest concern. Both tibias were shattered and there was some damage to the knee joints too. Bobby's hands had not escaped damage either, though the extent of their injury had yet to be assessed.

As she sat there, watching his motionless form, all kinds of thoughts went through Dee's mind. When he regained consciousness, what would his own reaction to his injuries be? Without asking she knew that there was a possibility that he might not walk normally again. And as for racing . . . She fought down her own anguish as she remembered her blatant dislike of his love of motorcycle racing and the way she had tried to get him to give it up; she thought of her decision to end their relationship. How could she tell him now? He would think she was abandoning him because of his injuries. The idea was unthinkable.

The curtains parted and Dee felt a gentle hand on her shoulder. 'Dee, come home, love.' It was Claire who stood looking down at her. 'I'm going off duty now. You can't do any more here. He'll probably be out for hours yet, and it's the best thing for him—you know that.'

Reluctantly, Dee got to her feet, realising for the first time how exhausted she was. She took one more look at Bobby, then turned and followed Claire back to the nurses' station at the centre of the ward, where the night staff were preparing to take over. A second-year nurse came in from the corridor and tapped Claire on the arm.

'Sister, Mr Carr's parents and his sister are waiting outside. Can they see him?'

Claire hesitated, turning to Dee. 'Perhaps you'd like to talk to them. Tell them they can slip in for a minute, one at a time, just to see him. Put them in the picture.'

Dee would have preferred not to, but she knew she could do no less.

In the small waiting room off the corridor George and Lena Carr waited, with Angie. They rose as Dee came in, looking anxiously towards her.

'You can slip in and see Bobby for a minute,' she told them. 'One at a time, if you don't mind. Don't worry, he's holding his own. He's going to be all right.'

Lena Carr stared at her with unconcealed hostility in her eyes. 'How can you stand there and glibly say that he's going to be all right?' she demanded. 'We were there at the track. We *saw* the accident. After what happened he'll be crippled for the rest of his life—you call *that* all right?' Her voice rose hysterically, and her husband laid a restraining hand on her arm.

'Steady, Lena, Deanne is only trying to reassure us. The boy's alive, and that's the important thing. We must cling to that for the moment.' He smiled apologetically at Dee as his wife swept out of the room. 'She's been under a lot of strain,' he said. 'It was terrible for her

—being there, seeing it happen like that. We thought he was . . .' he paused, reaching out to pat Dee's shoulder as he passed. 'Thank you, my dear.'

Dee nodded as he followed his wife out of the room. She looked at Angie, who asked softly: 'What are his chances, Dee? You can tell me.'

Dee shook her head. 'I only wish I *could* tell you. His internal injuries aren't too serious. But the shock, and loss of blood—his legs . . .' She glanced at Angie, wondering just how much she should tell her. 'Personally, what worries me most is his own reaction when he comes round and finds his legs so badly injured.'

'Was Mother right when she said he'd be crippled?' asked Angie.

Dee lifted her shoulders wearily. 'It's impossible to say at the moment. He'll need further surgery, of course—but so much will depend on his own attitude.'

Angie looked at her for a moment, then crossed the room to take both Dee's hands. 'Poor love,' she whispered. 'It must have been a horrific experience for you, being in the theatre when they brought him in. No one's given a thought to that, have they?'

Dee took a deep breath. Angie's kind words were the final straw and she felt the tears rising. 'I'm fine,' she insisted, trying to stop her lips from trembling. 'All I need is some rest. Bobby's the one to feel sorry for.'

Claire came in carrying Dee's coat. She slipped it round her friend's shoulders and, with a backward nod to Angie, led her firmly away. Back at the flat she made Dee eat something, then insisted she swallowed a sleeping tablet before tucking her up in bed.

The following morning the newspapers were full of the Grand Prix accident. Claire tactfully put them away out of Dee's sight. There were photographs of Bobby, taken before the race. There was one with his parents and another of Bobby with his arm round Geraldine. Underneath, the caption read: *A good-luck hug from girlfriend model Geraldine Moore*.

Since the previous evening the hospital had been besieged by reporters too, but the administrative staff took good care that they didn't disrupt the smooth running of the hospital's routine.

Dee slept late on Saturday morning. When she woke and looked at her bedside clock she was annoyed to find that it was after nine. She got up hurriedly. Slipping on her dressing gown, she went in search of Claire, taking her to task for not waking her. The other girl was unrepentant.

'You needed the rest. And anyway, you don't have to work today.'

'But Bobby! I must find out how he is,' Dee protested.

'He's doing fine,' Claire told her calmly. 'I telephoned to ask because I knew it would be the first thing you'd want to know. He had a good night and he's conscious and quite alert, though of course he'll still be heavily sedated. You can slip over and see him later. But first have some breakfast.'

Reluctantly, Dee allowed herself to be persuaded to sit down at the table and eat the breakfast Claire put in front of her. She felt better physically this morning, though her mental state was as bad as ever. As she drank a second cup of coffee she told Claire of the letter she had written to Bobby, breaking off their engagement. 'It was only to straighten my thoughts out that I wrote it,' she explained. 'I'll tear it up now. The situation's altered completely.' She got up to fetch her handbag.'

Claire frowned. 'What do you mean, the situation's altered?'

Dee looked up at her friend. 'Surely you can see that I can't tell him we're finished now! Imagine how it would look! I couldn't add to his troubles.'

'I see that, of course,' Claire said patiently. 'Right at this moment isn't a good time, but later—when he's recovered.'

Dee shook her head. 'You don't understand—I feel partly responsible. This was to be his last race. It was so important to him to win it. Maybe he tried too hard—took too many unnecessary risks.'

'From what I can gather it was pure accident,' Claire told her. 'Another racer crashed and Bobby wasn't able to avoid the wreckage. Taking risks didn't come into it.'

Dee shook her head. 'I don't know . . .' She was rummaging in her bag. Finally she tipped the contents of her handbag out on to the table and began to sort through them. At last she looked up at Claire, her eyes wide and her face drained of colour. 'The letter! It's not here! What can have happened . . . ?' Suddenly her mouth dropped open as she remembered colliding with Sister Fairchild as she was leaving the rest room the day before yesterday. She had dropped her bag. Sister had helped her to pick up the scattered contents. Somehow the letter must have escaped their notice—slipped under a chair or something. Another possibility occurred to her and her hand flew to her mouth. Suppose Sister had found the letter after she had gone—and *posted* it?

The words almost tumbling over each other, she confided her fears to Claire. 'It would have arrived yesterday morning—just before he left for the race,' she said. 'Maybe his mind was on that—maybe he wasn't concentrating as he should have been! Oh God, Claire, how *awful*!' She was shaking, and Claire reached across to touch her hand.

'Now wait a minute. Before you start panicking, why don't you just ring Mary Fairchild and ask her?'

Dee got up and went towards the kitchen to telephone —but halfway across the room she stopped. 'I can't! She's on leave for two weeks. She told me yesterday that she was catching the night train to Edinburgh to spend a couple of weeks with her sister!'

The two girls stood staring at each other, momentarily at a loss, then Claire said: 'Can't you get her sister's name from records? Surely there must be some way.'

But there wasn't. Sister Fairchild's next of kin was her mother, who lived in London; and as her sister was married and no one knew her married name there was no way they could trace her.

'It's no use,' said Claire at last. 'You'll just have to play it by ear.' She didn't say so, but she assumed that Bobby would tell her if he had received the letter. The same thought occurred to Dee, but she too remained silent, shrinking from the prospect.

She showered and pulled on jeans and a sweater, then went across to the hospital and took the lift up to Intensive Care. Bobby was still on a drip, but he was breathing without the aid of the ventilator this morning and, as Claire had told her, he was conscious and, though still sedated, he was fairly alert. He smiled at her.

'Hi.'

She took a seat at his bedside and touched one bandaged arm gently. 'How are you feeling?'

'Rough. There doesn't seem to be square inch of me that doesn't hurt like hell, though I guess it'd be worse if it wasn't for the dope they've stuffed me with.' He looked at her hesitantly. 'Were you there—when they brought me in, I mean?'

'Yes. I was there in the theatre when they patched you up.'

'I'm relying on you, Dee, to tell me the score. No one here will tell me a damned thing. Might as well let me have it—what have I done?'

Dee took a deep breath, knowing that it would be useless to try to stall him. 'Your—your legs were injured in the crash.'

'Oddly enough, I'd gathered that,' Bobby told her wryly. 'And I suspect it's the understatement of the year.' He frowned. 'You know, it's funny, but yesterday is a complete blank. I can't even remember waking up! It's as though I went to bed on Thursday night and woke up in here. Odd, isn't it?'

Inwardly she breathed a sigh of relief. If he remembered nothing about yesterday he wouldn't remember getting her letter. At least she had a breathing space. 'Just as well,' she told him. 'The memories could hardly be pleasant ones.'

She hadn't been there for more than five minutes when Greig arrived. She got up to leave, but he motioned to her to stay while he made a brief examination of Bobby's legs.

Bobby watched the surgeon's face carefully all the time, and when the examination was over he said: 'I want you to tell me the worst, Doc. No pussyfooting round—I can take it.'

Greig drew up a chair and sat down, looking thoughtfully at the young man in the bed. 'You're lucky,' he said frankly. 'In the first place to be alive and in the second place to have both your legs still. If it hadn't been for those heavily padded leathers you were wearing we might have had no choice but to amputate. Another thing—the fracture you had a while back left you with scarred bone which resisted splintering better than it might have done otherwise.'

Bobby was searching the surgeon's eyes shrewdly. 'Okay, so that's the good news. What about the bad?'

Greig glanced at Dee, then went on: 'There's a large area of fragmentation below each knee at the top of the tibia—that's the shinbone.' He nodded towards the heavily bandaged hands. 'And I don't have to tell you that your hands and wrists caught a lot of the impact. There's some pretty extensive work for us there too.'

'So what happens? Take the legs first—do I wind up a foot shorter than before, or what?' Bobby was making a brave effort, but Dee knew him well enough to know that behind the brittle facetiousness he was very scared—and who could blame him?

Greig shook his head. 'As soon as you've had a good rest I intend to operate. I promise you I'll do my very best to make you as good as new.'

'But if the bones are shattered . . . ?'

'There are ways and means,' Greig interrupted. 'You can let me worry about the mechanics.'

Bobby's blue eyes were very bright as he asked: 'Will I be able to race again?'

The question shook them both. Greig flashed a look at Dee and they exchanged a glance of pure amazement. Greig's eyes darkened with a lightning flash of anger as he returned his gaze to Bobby and said briskly: 'Just thank God you're alive, Mr Carr—and pray to God that you'll get back the normal use in those legs. If you do, I think you should consider it a gift not to be lightly gambled with!' He got to his feet and Bobby asked quickly:

'When are you going to do it—the op?'

Greig turned to look at him. 'When I'm satisfied that you're fit.' He strode from the cubicle, and Bobby looked pleadingly at Dee.

'Quick, go after him and see what you can find out. He'll tell you,' he urged.

She did as he asked, mainly because she had a dozen questions of her own to ask. 'I'll be back later,' she told Bobby. 'Try to get as much rest as you can.'

Greig was walking very fast and she had to run to catch him up. They were almost at the end of the corridor and he had his hand on the door when she called: 'Greig —wait, please!' He turned to look at her. 'I'd like to have a word with you—about Bobby.'

He looked down at her. In her hastily donned jeans and sweater and with her hair tied back she looked so young that his heart twisted. He had lain awake thinking of her for most of last night, haunted by her shocked white face in the theatre as she struggled to carry out her work normally; despising himself for wondering what difference this new development might make to what she felt for Bobby Carr. He hesitated briefly, knowing full well that it was the worst kind of folly to allow himself to become involved, then said: 'You'd better come along to my office. We'll talk there.'

The lift was crowded and they exchanged neither word nor look. In his office Greig closed the door and indicated a chair. 'Sit down—you look all in. Did you sleep?'

She nodded. 'Claire gave me a sleeping tablet. I feel a bit hung over this morning, though. Greig . . .' she leaned forward, 'tell me the truth—how much are you going to be able to do for Bobby?'

He took out the X-ray pictures and clipped the first of them on to the viewing screen. It showed Bobby's shattered tibias and damaged knee joints. Dee winced. 'Dear God! What can you do?'

He snapped off the light. 'I've seen worse—but not *much* worse, I admit. I *can* restructure, but whether or not he walks normally again will be largely up to him.' He sat down and looked at her. 'I don't have to tell you, Dee, that he's in for a hell of a lot of pain. The recovery and the physiotherapy will be agony. Lesser men than him have been known to give up.'

She sighed. 'So he's going to need all the support he can get. That's what you're saying, isn't it?'

'Of course, but then he isn't short of friends and he has his family.' He looked at her for a long moment, losing an inward battle with the question that refused to go away. 'Dee, maybe I shouldn't ask this, but—are you going to let what's happened alter things between you and Bobby?'

I—don't know.' Her eyes slid away from his and she stared down at her hands. 'I—did something the other day, Greig,' she said haltingly. 'I wrote a letter. Oh, not to send—just to clarify my own feelings—to work out what I'd say to Bobby. I was waiting till after the race. I thought he wouldn't mind too much after it was over, specially if he won.'

'What are you trying to say?' His eyes were dark as they looked into hers.

Dee took a deep breath. 'I can't find the letter. I think I must have dropped it and I'm terribly afraid that someone may have picked it up and posted it for me. If that were the case, he would have got it yesterday morning before the race.'

'Have you asked him if he received it?'

She shook her head. 'Yesterday is a total blank. He says he doesn't even remember getting up. He has no recollection of the race—the accident—nothing.'

Greig nodded. 'That's quite usual in cases like this. It'll probably all come back bit by bit, but at least it gives you time to think.'

Dee shook her head impatiently. 'Don't you see, Greig? *I* may have caused the accident!' The green eyes were wide with anguish as they looked into his. 'I feel I owe Bobby so much now. I have to try to make up to him. Because of me he may be . . .'

'*Dee!*' His voice was hard as he interrupted her. 'You're letting your emotions run away with you! Bobby's accident couldn't possibly have been your fault. Nothing's changed. You're the same two people you were yesterday.' He flung out his hands. 'You heard what he asked me—*Will I be able to race again?* Doesn't *that* tell you anything? Or do you think he's forgotten his promise to you too?'

She frowned, her head spinning with confusion. 'I don't *know*!' All I do know at the moment is that I have to be there if he needs me.' She looked up at him. 'And when he's well again—if he still wants to marry me—even if he goes back to racing . . .'

'Don't be a fool, Dee!' Greig got up and came round the desk to stand looking down at her. 'You'd be ruining your life. You know that, don't you? If he makes it—races again, you'd be living daily with the possibility of another accident, and if not . . .'

'I've thought of all that.'

'Then what?' He grasped her arm and dragged her to her feet. 'You love him more than you thought, is that it? Love him enough to throw your life at his feet, no matter what happens?'

Dee felt the tears begin to well up behind her eyes as she shook her head. 'That doesn't come into it, Greig. I can't do less, can't you *see*?'

'No, damn it, I *can't* see! If you didn't love him enough to marry him before then you shouldn't be contemplating it now—*especially* not now!' He was gripping her shoulders, looking down at her intently, but when he saw her face crumple, heard the stifled sob in her throat, his heart contracted and he pulled her into his arms. He wanted to tell her that he'd do anything in the world to prevent her from getting hurt—that the thought of her throwing herself away was tearing him apart. Most of all he wanted to tell her that he loved her, but he knew this was neither the time nor the place. He knew too, with a crushing certainty, that the time and place for telling her these things might never come. While the tumult raged in his heart he remained silent, rocking her gently and stroking her hair until her sobs subsided. Then he asked her softly: 'What do you want me to do, Dee? Just tell me how can I help you?'

She longed to beg him to go on holding her like

this—warm and safe. Wanted to beg him to take her somewhere far away and wipe out all that had happened over the last twenty-four hours, but none of this was possible. Instead she said, looking up at him: 'Just make him whole again. I'll try to do the rest.'

It was an ambiguous statement, and he cupped her chin and looked searchingly into her eyes. 'For God's sake, Dee, think about yourself a little—think about what you're doing and all the consequences,' he whispered. 'Before it's too late . . .' Their eyes met and locked for a long anguished moment. He felt the irresistible draw of her, pulling him like a magnet, and although he tried to fight it his head bent towards hers—but at the moment their lips met there came a loud knock on the door, startling them both back to reality. Greig's arms dropped from her and she turned, trembling, to gather up her handbag from his desk as he called: 'Come in.'

The door opened to reveal Lena Carr. 'I'm sorry to disturb you, Mr Meredith . . .' Then she saw Dee and a surprised, slightly shocked expression wiped the smile from her face. 'Oh, Deanne!'

Dee began to move towards the door, but Greig grasped her arm and held her fast. 'It's Mrs Carr, isn't it?' he said pleasantly. 'I expect you want to talk about your son. Please come in.'

Lena stepped into the room and stared pointedly at Dee. Greig went on: 'You know Nurse Latimer, of course. She was in the theatre with me last night when your son had his emergency operation. Under the circumstances it was an extremely harrowing experience for her.'

Lena looked at him coldly. '*I* was at the track and witnessed my son's accident,' she told him. 'That was even more harrowing!'

Greig pulled out a chair for her. 'Of course—it must

have been terrible for you. Please sit down, Mrs Carr, and tell me what I can do for you.'

Lena settled herself in the chair Greig offered, then, without further preamble, she said: 'My husband and I feel it's time something was done for Bobby.'

If Greig was annoyed he didn't show it. 'In what way, Mrs Carr?'

Lena gave a sharp little laugh. 'I should have thought that was obvious! We'd like to know what you intend to do for him—and *when*?'

'I'm fairly confident that I shall be able to help your son quite a lot with surgery,' Greig told her guardedly. 'I hope to operate as soon as possible.'

'Which is . . . ?' Lena's tone was challenging, and Dee saw Greig's colour deepen slightly.

'Possibly tomorrow. If not, then almost certainly on Monday.'

'Not good enough. We would like it done immediately!' Lena got to her feet. 'We intend to have him moved to a private hospital as soon as we can arrange a bed, probably this afternoon,' she told him. 'And when I tell you that we're willing to pay privately for his operation no doubt you'll change your mind about its urgency!'

Greig got to his feet and Dee could see that he was extremely angry. Although his expression conveyed little of what he was feeling there was a white line around his mouth and dangerous flecks of green flashed in his eyes as he replied: 'I must warn you, Mrs Carr, that if you remove your son from this hospital I cannot be held responsible for his welfare—furthermore, I shall not operate on him unless he remains where he is. At present he is not fit to be moved or to be operated on. When he is, I shall perform his operation to the best of my ability.' He took her arm and guided her towards the door where he turned to her and said: 'I think I should

tell you that I do not accept private patients, Mrs Carr.
Nor do I take orders from patients' relatives. Your
son will receive the same care and attention and the
same skills as any other patient. If you find this unsatis-
factory you are, naturally, at liberty to make your own
arrangements.'

But Lena wasn't to be put down. Her cold blue eyes
were like chips of ice as she flung one last parting shot at
him: 'What about the MP you treated? *You're not
expecting me to believe you weren't paid a pretty penny
for that!* Or was all the publicity enough for you?'

Dee held her breath. She had always known that
Bobby's mother was an unpleasant woman, but this
. . . ! Greig's control astonished her as he said calmly: 'I
can only repeat what I've just told you, Mrs Carr. If
your son remains where he is I shall do everything
in my power for him. If you insist on removing him
against my advice it will be up to you to find another
surgeon.'

As he closed the door firmly on the furious woman he
let out his breath in an explosive hiss and turned to Dee,
his eyes blazing with unleashed anger and his fists
clenched. 'God almighty! And to think *that's* the woman
you're contemplating as your mother-in-law!'

For a moment they stared at each other, then the glint
of fury died in Greig's eyes and his shoulders began to
shake. To her surprise Dee saw that he was laughing.
Relieved, she joined in, going to him and taking both his
hands in hers. The release of tension was almost overwhelming and soon they were clinging to each other,
laughing helplessly, until suddenly their eyes met—held
—and the laughter stopped abruptly. Wiping the tears
from her cheeks with his fingertips, Greig drew her
slowly to him, and as his lips met hers Dee caught her
breath. What on earth was the matter with her? Was she
going mad? First laughing hysterically as though

Bobby's accident were some grotesque joke—now letting Greig kiss her like this! Not only allowing it but wanting it with all her heart. Suddenly the whole world seemed to be standing on its head. It was like some crazy mixed-up dream—and just about as impossible! The kiss ended as abruptly as it had begun and Greig put her firmly from him, looking down at her apologetically, his hands on her shoulders. 'Off you go and get some lunch,' he told her gruffly. 'And remind me to keep out of that woman's way from now on!' Silently, to himself he added: 'And out of yours too—my darling!'

CHAPTER EIGHT

THAT afternoon Dee sat once again at Bobby's bedside. He had been moved from Intensive Care now and, at his mother's insistence, placed in a small private room. But though he had been cheerful that morning he was now more subdued. Now that the previous evening's anaesthetic and the heavy sedation administered that morning had worn off he was in a great deal of pain, and he rolled his head restlessly on the pillow as Dee looked on helplessly. There was so little she could do. Even his hands were heavily bandaged, and contact of any kind obviously hurt him.

'This time tomorrow your op will be over,' she told him encouragingly. 'Greig—Mr Meredith is confident he can restructure your legs. After that it will be up to you.'

Bobby turned his head to look at her. 'Great! That's *really* something to look forward to!'

She shook her head at his obvious bitterness. 'I know you're going through a lot, Bobby, but everyone here is doing all they can for you. We're all behind you.'

He frowned impatiently at her. 'I know—I *know*.' He tried to shift his position and winced. 'You know, the only thing that's making any of this hell bearable is the thought of getting back on that track again. It's the one thing I'm hanging on to. I know what I promised, but it's no good, Dee. If I can't . . .' He closed his eyes, groaning a little, and she took a tissue from the box on his locker and wiped the beads of perspiration from his brow.

'You're tiring yourself out. Don't talk any more,' she told him.

'When do I get the next shot?' He opened his eyes to look at her.

Dee got up to look at his chart, then glanced at her watch. 'Not for another hour, I'm afraid.'

'God! As long as that?—Hasn't anyone around this place got any feelings? I don't know if I can take much more of this!'

She got up to switch on the television in the corner of the room. 'How about watching TV for a while?' she suggested cheerfully. 'It's sport on Saturday afternoons, isn't it?'

'Okay, okay. Anything to help take my mind off it,' Bobby sighed resignedly.

Footsteps and voices were heard outside in the corridor and a moment later the door opened to reveal Bobby's parents and Angie. Dee turned to smile at Bobby.

'Well, you have visitors now, so I'll go.' She slipped out into the corridor, avoiding Mrs Carr's eyes, but she had gone only a few yards when she heard someone call her, and turning, she saw Angie and George Carr following her.

'Could we have a word with you, Dee?' asked Angie.

Dee hesitated. 'Well—yes, of course.' She glanced around. 'Better come into the waiting room.'

As luck would have it the room was empty and all three sat down. George Carr came straight to the point: 'I'm afraid my wife was very rude to Mr Meredith this morning. I believe you were present at the time.'

Dee shrugged dismissively. She was embarrassed, hoping they weren't going to question her about the heated exchange. 'She's been under a great strain,' she said. 'I'm sure he understood.'

But George sighed. 'Nevertheless, she should have

tried to curb her impatience. If we can't trust Meredith's judgment as to the right time to operate, whose can we trust? I tried to contact him, but he wasn't available.' He smiled wryly. 'Hardly surprising after Lena's outburst.' He leaned towards her. 'As you were there I wondered if you'd do us a favour and convey our apologies to him. Tell him that we have the greatest confidence in him. After all, he's got a good name for this kind of thing, hasn't he?'

Dee gave him a warning look. 'I wouldn't mention that to him if I were you. He hates publicity and media hype. He's a very good man, Mr Carr, in every sense of the word, and I can assure you that he'll do his very best for Bobby, just as he would for anyone else.' She saw Angie flash her a curious look and felt her cheeks colour slightly. 'It isn't going to be easy for Bobby,' she went on, avoiding the other girl's eyes. 'He has a great ordeal ahead of him in the coming weeks. He'll need all the help and encouragement he can get. But I'm sure he'll get it from all of you.'

George Carr got to his feet and laid a hand on her shoulder. 'You can rely on it. So you'll try to smooth things over for us, will you—with Meredith, I mean?'

Dee nodded. 'I'll do my best.'

He glanced at his watch. 'Right, I'll go in and see the boy now. I'm sure Lena will be most grateful to you, my dear.'

Dee felt equally sure that Lena would be nothing of the kind. She would be furious if she knew that Dee had been asked to make apologies for her. But she kept her thoughts to herself.

Bobby's father walked to the door. 'Are you coming?' he was addressing Angie, but she shook her head. 'Better not crowd him. I'll look in for a couple of minutes when you leave.' When her father had gone she looked at Dee.

'Are you all right?'

Dee nodded. 'It's been a very traumatic time. Were you at the track yesterday?'

'Yes. It was horrific. We didn't actually see the crash—there was too much smoke around at the time. But wondering if it was Bobby and how badly he was hurt—then afterwards when we knew, when we saw him . . .' She shuddered. 'I wouldn't like to have to live through that again.'

'If he comes through this successfully you may have to—we may all have to,' Dee told her. 'He's made it quite clear that he intends racing again if it's at all possible.'

Angie's eyes widened. 'He can't be serious!'

'He is, I assure you.'

'And—if—if it isn't successful . . . ?'

Dee bit her lip. 'We're not even going to think about that.'

'He promised you he'd give up,' Angie said. 'How do you feel about his going back on his word?'

Dee shrugged. 'I'm sure you must feel as I do—we have to be thankful that Bobby is alive. That fact seems to make everything else unimportant, doesn't it?' She looked hard at the other girl. 'Angie, do you know whether anything happened to upset Bobby before the race?'

The other girl shook her head. 'He seemed in great spirits as far as I could tell. Why?'

'I—just wondered.'

'You two hadn't quarrelled again, had you?'

'No. I just wondered if there could have been any reason for his accident—other than pure mishap.'

The other girl looked at her closely. 'What's on your mind, Dee?'

'Nothing—it's just that I wondered, that's all.' Dee sighed. 'I should never have asked Bobby to give up racing. It meant too much to him . . .'

Angie was looking at her intently. She was perceptive enough to know that there was something more than Bobby's accident and impending operation worrying her. The look in her eyes when she had spoken about the orthopaedic consultant, the quick way she had risen to his defence, hadn't escaped her notice either. Could it be that . . . ? But she decided not to probe the matter further. Anyway, it was really none of her business. She reached out a hand to Dee.

'Don't worry about it, love. The next few days will be crucial. We must take them one at a time and hope for a full recovery for Bobby. As you say, nothing else matters—at the moment anyway.' There was a pause as Angie looked sympathetically at her. 'Dee,' she began, 'this is a traumatic situation, but you mustn't let yourself make the wrong decision just because . . .' The door opened and a group of visitors came in, putting an end to the conversation. Outside in the corridor Angie laid a hand on Dee's arm. 'Look, love; if you need someone to talk to you know where I am. Don't make a lot of rash promises—and don't *do* anything rash, will you? Bobby's future may be in the balance, but your life is important too.' She smiled. 'And you won't forget your promise to Dad, will you?'

'I won't—and, Angie . . . ' Dee looked into the other girl's eyes, 'you won't mention any of what I've told you to anyone, will you?'

Angie gave her a reproachful look. 'What do you take me for?'

Greig wasn't in his office, and Dee walked back to Wedgwood House. It was Saturday afternoon. If he had any sense he would be out somewhere, enjoying the warm sunshine, she told herself. Maybe he'd even driven up to London to a concert or theatre.

Outside his flat she lifted her hand and knocked hesitantly on the door. There was a long pause, then she heard his voice from inside: 'Who is it?'

Slightly taken aback, she answered: 'It's me—Dee Latimer.'

He opened the door and looked at her apologetically. 'Sorry about that. I thought it might be those damned reporters again. I gave them an interview this morning on the advice of the HA, but it doesn't seem to have taken the heat off. They seem to pop up everywhere. It seems that Bobby Carr is suddenly hot news.' He gave her a wry grin. 'You'd better watch it. They'll be after you if you're not careful!'

Dee winced. 'Oh no! That's all I need.'

He looked enquiringly at her. 'What can I do for you?'

'It's just that I saw Mr Carr, Bobby's father, up on the ward just now,' she told him. 'He asked me to apologise for his wife's outburst to you this morning. I promised I would. He wants you to know that he's happy to put his trust in you.'

Greig's eyebrows rose. 'Very big of him! Apology accepted.' He smiled at her. 'Thanks for delivering it.'

'I'd been sitting with Bobby,' she told him. 'He's in rather a lot of pain and pretty depressed. Have you decided when you're going to operate?'

He nodded. 'Tomorrow morning, if all goes well. I'll be going up to see him again this evening. Sunday seems a good day for it. I won't have a full list pushing me.'

'Will it be a long job?' she asked.

He considered for a moment. 'Be lucky to get away with it under eight hours.'

'May I help?' she asked. 'Scrub for you?'

His eyebrows shot up. 'But you're not even on duty tomorrow.'

'I could swap with Nurse Hall. She surely won't mind having a Sunday off.'

'Sorry, I can't allow it.'

'But why?'

'You're too involved.'

'But I won't let you down—pass out or anything. If I was going to do that I'd have done it yesterday . . .'

'I said no!'

Dee stared at him. His tone made it clear that it was no use to argue. 'Can I observe, then?' she asked. 'From the viewing room? Please—I won't get in the way. Can I say I have your permission?'

Greig sighed and lifted his shoulders. 'All right, then, if you must.'

'Thanks.' Suddenly there seemed nothing more to say. She turned. 'Well, I suppose I'd better go.'

He walked with her to the door, searching his mind for a reason to ask her to stay. As his hand touch the door handle the excuse he was looking for suddenly dropped into his mind. 'What are you going to do with the rest of the afternoon?' he asked.

She looked up at him in surprise. 'Me?—nothing. Bobby has his family with him.' She lifted her shoulders. 'I dare say I can find a job upstairs in the flat. There's always something that needs doing.'

'Come and look at a house with me instead.' He crossed the room and took an envelope from the mantelpiece. Drawing out a leaflet, he handed it to her. 'I had this from the estate agents this morning. It looks rather intriguing. I'd appreciate your opinion.' He looked at her enquiringly.

She laughed. 'Mine? I don't know anything about property.'

'Why not come anyway? It'll help take your mind off things here.'

Suddenly her heart lifted. It was a beautiful day. She could do with some fresh air and she loved looking at houses. Inwardly she gave herself half a dozen plausible, innocent reasons to accept Greig's invitation—every one she could think of except the one nearest the truth. 'Well—all right. Yes, I'd like that. Just give me ten minutes to wash and change.' As she ran up the stairs to the flat it was as though her feet had wings.

Standing in his doorway Greig watched her, his heart full of misgivings. What the hell did he think he was doing? Playing with fire! At his age he should have known better! And after all his resolutions not to see her. The house the agents had sent him details of had sounded quite impossibly unsuitable. He had tossed it aside after one look at the leaflet. A neglected Georgian house with five bedrooms, in the country, eight miles from the hospital, was about the last place he'd choose to live. But however hard he upbraided himself he couldn't quite quell the thrill of anticipation of the afternoon ahead; several hours shared with Dee. Just being with her couldn't do any harm, surely? he reasoned. Even if it was under false pretences.

Bobby closed his eyes, relaxing a little as the Pethidine injected a few minutes ago by the staff nurse began to take effect. What had he done to deserve such stinking luck? he asked himself bitterly. He'd been so sure that the Grand Prix was his. So had everyone else. When he thought of all the practice he'd put in—all the hard work rebuilding the bike, and all for this! Scalding tears stung his eyes as he lay blinking up at the ceiling. If it hadn't been for that bloody fool taking the bend too wide . . . He'd insisted on getting his father to describe the accident for him, to fill him in on exactly what had happened. It wouldn't be so bad if he remembered, but the whole day was a complete blank. He visualised the scene—imagined his lifeless form being lifted on to a stretcher and placed in the ambulance; rushed here and taken to the operating theatre to be patched up like some old crock. The thought made him feel sick. He had always found illness and injury repulsive. He thought of Dee seeing him like that, stretched out on a slab like a dead carcass, and shrank with disgust and humiliation. She'd always hated bikes and racing. Maybe she thought he'd stop now—now that he'd have no choice but to live the kind of life she wanted him to. Then there were his parents. In spite of their concern and sympathy this afternoon there was no concealing what they really felt. They were thinking they'd got him back again—under their control. It was only a matter of time now before he would be chairbound—preferably at his father's desk! Suddenly he knew how it felt to be a trapped animal —imagined himself with his legs caught fast between those vicious steel jaws, the predatory faces of his captors leering triumphantly down at him. 'That's your lot, boy! That's put a stop to your fun and games!'

'*Mr Carr!* Are you all right?'

He hadn't been aware that he'd cried out, and he grinned sheepishly at the young nurse who looked anxiously in at him. 'I think I must have nodded off—I was dreaming. Sorry, Nurse.'

She straightened his sheet, fussing a little over the corners. 'That's all right. Try to get some sleep. You're going to need all your strength for tomorrow.'

She left him alone and he closed his eyes. *All his strength*. He gritted his teeth. She could say that again! He'd get back on that race track if it was the last thing he did. Out of this trap and back on the bike—or bloody well die in the attempt.

'I didn't know you were looking for a house.' Dee sat beside Greig as they drove out of town and into the gently undulating Northamptonshire countryside.

'I wasn't.' He smiled ruefully, his eyes on the road. 'I fully intended to make that flat my home until I thought about it. For one thing, it's a bit like living over the shop and for another, it isn't fair to take up hospital accommodation when there are others who need it more.'

'I see.' She glanced at him. 'But won't you find it rather lonely?'

'Shan't know till I try, will I?' He looked at her. 'If I do I can always find someone to share it with—take in paying guests or something.' He peered at a signpost. 'Ah, Little Gresham two miles. I think this is the turning. Will you look at the instructions on the leaflet for me again?'

The house stood at the end of a quiet lane on the fringe of the village. According to the leaflet it had been built somewhere around the end of the eighteenth century. Square and solid-looking, it stood in its own grounds, surrounded by tall yew hedges. A white-painted five-barred gate set into an attractive stone wall gave on to a circular drive with a cedar tree in the centre. Greig stopped the car and looked at Dee.

'Well, this is it. What do you think?'

'It's a mansion in miniature,' she said delightedly. 'Just like a doll's house. I love that mellow rose-pink brick and the lovely rustic-looking roof—what's it made of?'

Greig looked in the leaflet. 'Collyweston slate, it says here. I think that's a local quarry.' He released his seat belt. 'Shall we go and explore?'

They had picked up the key at the estate agent's office on the way. As they walked up the drive Dee looked around her at the overgrown garden borders. 'Mmm, no one's lived here for some time, by the look of things. I hope you enjoy gardening.'

'Brought up on it,' he told her. 'I told you, didn't I? My father's an expert.' He followed her gaze. 'Time would be the only snag.' He inserted the key in the lock of the front door and pushed it open. The hall was square and spacious with a stone-flagged floor. An open-well staircase led to the first floor, and Dee exclaimed with delight at the Venetian window on the half-landing, through which streamed the afternoon sunlight.

'Oh, isn't this pretty!'

Greig looked doubtfully at the chipped brown paint-work and peeling, faded wallpaper. 'Is it?'

'Oh *yes*!' She looked around her. 'If the walls were stripped and re-papered in a warm colour—perhaps an ivory satin-striped paper. And with the woodwork painted white it would make all the difference. You could have it carpeted in wine red or maybe a rich gold . . .' She bounced ahead of him, opening the sturdy panelled doors to peep into the rooms. There were three reception rooms and a maze of sculleries and pantries which Dee announced should all be knocked into one large cosy kitchen-cum-breakfast room with an adjoining utility.

'Can't you just see it?' she asked him, her eyes bright with enthusiasm. 'There'd be a huge Welsh dresser over there on that wall, all decked out with Willow Pattern china, copper pans and a big table in the middle. Oh, and a rocking chair by the fireplace. There'd *have* to be a rocking chair!'

He looked amused. 'What about all those microwave oven things and washing machines most women seem to feel are vital?'

Dee waved a dismissive hand. 'Oh, you can have them conveniently hidden away somewhere. This would be a homely, old-fashioned kitchen.'

He raised an enquiring eyebrow. 'That suggests a homely, old-fashioned wife! Any suggestions where I can find one?'

The enthusiasm faded from her eyes as she looked up at him. 'I'm sorry, I was getting carried away, wasn't I?

My ideas wouldn't be at all practical for a bachelor living alone. You must think me really silly.' She began to move away, but he caught at her arm.

'Of course I don't think you're silly. You're right about your ideas not being practical for me, but I'm enjoying hearing them all the same.' He looked down at her, his eyes warm. 'It's good to see you smiling again, and it's refreshing to be with someone so optimistic.' He clasped her hand warmly and led her towards the hall again. 'Come on, let's take a look upstairs and see what horrors are lurking up there!'

There were four large bedrooms, all with pleasant views of the garden, and a tiny one which Dee speculated might have been intended as a dressing room or maybe a nursery. The bathroom was a nightmare of rusting antique plumbing, festooned with a tangle of pipes. Over the bath loomed a monstrous-looking geyser which Greig tapped sharply with his knuckles. Dee gave a scream of alarm as, along with a shower of rust, a large spider dropped to the floor and ran across her foot. He laughed. 'I'd say there was a little modernisation work to be done in here,' he said. 'What is your fancy, madame—a circular bath in pink marble —maybe a matching sauna? Or do you favour a jacuzzi?' He raised a quizzical eyebrow at her.

'I see it in warm sunrise yellow and pine,' she told him, half closing her eyes. 'With a deep, soft creamy carpet and lots of fluffy cream towels warming on a heated rail. Over there, a shower cubicle and lots of green ferns everywhere.'

He sucked in his cheeks and regarded her, his head on one side. 'If I didn't know what a good nurse you are I'd say you were in the wrong job, girl. I've half a mind to buy this place and let you loose in it.' He laughed. 'The only thing that's stopping me is that you'd bankrupt me before you'd half finished!' He walked out on to the landing and began to descend the stairs.

Dee followed him, slightly puzzled. Surely his salary as a consultant would have run to it? 'It needn't cost all that much,' she told him. 'You could do a lot of the work yourself.'

He looked over his shoulder. 'Pop over here in between operations, you mean?'

'No. During your holidays—time off—weekends.'

'It would take years to do it that way. Besides which it's probably unsound structurally. No, I think it's got to be the traditional bijou residence for me, somewhere in the green belt within easy reach of everything.' They reached the hall again and stood looking round, their voices echoing slightly in the emptiness.

Dee sighed. 'I suppose you're right. Oh, but it *would* be fun!' There was a wistful note to her voice. The house was just the kind she had always dreamed of living in herself. She thought of the comfortable small suburban house she had grown up in with her parents. That had been sold after the divorce and her father now lived in an impersonal shoe-box of a flat. Seeing this house had brought home to her how much she missed having a real home.

Sensing her wistfulness, Greig reached out to touch her cheek. 'Cheer up, sweetheart. It was fun looking anyway. Let's go and get some tea, shall we? Tell you what—we'll find a place where they do homemade cream cakes and make utter pigs of ourselves.'

They found just such a place in the nearby village and sat for an hour over tea, scones and cream cakes, talking in a relaxed way about houses. Greig described to her the little terraced house he had grown up in along with his large family. It seemed they had been desperately overcrowded. He hadn't known what it was to have a room of his own until he had left home to go to university. 'But it was the happiest place on earth,' he told her.

'If I close my eyes I can still smell the fragrance of newly baked bread in the kitchen on Mam's baking days, or the sweet smell of clean linen when she was ironing.' He smiled at the memory. 'My dad took me down the pit on my tenth birthday. He said he wanted me to see what it was like so that I'd always remember and be thankful I'd worked hard for a better life.' He shook his head, his eyes soft with reminiscence. 'Many's the time I've remembered those words of his since the accident that ended his working life for good.'

It came out after that that Greig had bought his father a bungalow and paid for it to be adapted for life in a wheelchair so that he could be independent. Although he didn't say so, Dee guessed that Greig was probably also supplementing his father's pension too, which would account for his remarks about affording the house. She looked at the hands that rested on the table; strong, broad, capable hands, with long sensitive fingers. Skilful, talented hands. Suddenly she found herself wanting to meet Greig's brave, hardworking father. 'He must be very proud of you,' she said softly. 'I'd like to meet him.'

He looked startled for a moment. '*Would* you?' He smiled. 'He'd like you—he's always been keen on redheads. Maybe . . .' He stopped, looking at his watch. 'Come on, girl, time we were getting back.' He got to his feet. 'I have a patient to check on.'

Bobby dozed fitfully in his small room, the lights dimmed. He was feeling low, exhausted by the pain and the effort of being cheerful for his family, his mind depressed at the prospect of what lay ahead. When the door opened and Greig came in accompanied by the Ward Sister and Dr Brian James, the anaesthetist, he groaned. More proddings and pokings. Why the hell couldn't they leave him alone? Why didn't they just give him a triple dose of that dope and let him snuff it peacefully?

Dr James carefully examined his chest and took his blood pressure, then nodded his approval to Greig, who was studying the chart that hung on the end of the bed. He made a gentle and careful examination of the damaged legs. No further complications. As far as he could see tomorrow morning would be ideal for the operation. He nodded to Sister, who carefully unbandaged the hands. They promised to be an even greater challenge than the legs, but at least the thickly padded gloves had saved them from severe external injury, which was a blessing. 'You've sent blood for cross-matching, have you, Sister?' he asked, clipping the chart back into position. She affirmed that she had and he smiled at his patient. 'Well, I'm sure you'll be glad to hear that we're going to operate tomorrow morning, Mr Carr,' he announced. 'This time tomorrow we'll have you back together again.'

Bobby looked up at him. 'I've got to be able to race again, Doc. Do you understand? If you can't make me as good as new you might as well finish me off here and now.'

Greig's lips tightened. 'You mean that after all my work you'll go right out there and risk this kind of injury again?'

Bobby nodded, the ghost of his old enthusiasm glimmering in his eyes. 'Haven't you seen the papers? I've never been so popular! After this I'll be the greatest draw in the country. I'm made! Just fix me up and I'll make *your* name as well as mine!'

The light in Bobby's eyes almost submerged the look of pain, and for this reason Greig bit back a reproach. 'It doesn't all rest with me, you know,' he said bluntly. 'The operation to rebuild your legs is only the beginning. It'll mean damned hard work for you when I've finished.

And you start tomorrow, right from the moment you come round. It'll be no picnic, I can assure you,' he warned. 'It'll hurt like all hell let loose and take what'll seem like forever. I hope you feel it's worth it!'

Bobby summoned the ghost of a grin. 'You bet I do!'

'Right. See you in the morning, then.' Grim-faced, Greig turned on his heel and walked out of the room, his mind seething with a mixture of anger and sadness. Anger for the young man with what seemed to him like a death-wish, and sadness for the girl who had blindly pledged herself to him—the girl he no longer even tried to deny that he loved. 'What a waste,' he muttered to himself. 'What a damned *criminal* waste!'

CHAPTER NINE

DEE walked back to the flat through the deserted Sunday morning streets. Unable to sleep, she had risen early and gone out to buy Sunday papers; the one with the colour supplement that she and Claire always read and another, chosen because of the picture of Bobby on the front page and the startling headline: *'Promising young motorcycle racer may lose leg!'* She wondered where they had got their information from. Or was it that mere restructuring surgery wasn't sensational enough for them?

Back at the flat she put the kettle on, glancing at the clock. It was still early; she would let Claire sleep on for a while. She opened the paper with the picture of Bobby and spread it on the kitchen table. The centre pages carried a feature on Bobby's career in racing, complete with pictures of him: Bobby with various successive bikes; with his parents and Angie and, in the centre of the page, the latest shot, taken of him just before the race on Friday, with his arm around a smiling Geraldine Moore. The caption: *Carr with glamorous girl-friend, model Gerry Moore.* Underneath was a short interview with Geraldine, who told of how she and Bobby had been childhood sweethearts and of her deep concern for him. Dee closed the paper quickly and tossed it aside in disgust. If Geraldine Moore was so bothered about Bobby why hadn't she been anywhere near the hospital since he was admitted on Friday? No doubt all this was doing her modelling career so much good that she hadn't the time! She turned to the boiling kettle to make the tea.

She was just putting cups and saucers on to a tray

when the door opened and a sleepy-eyed Claire walked into the kitchen. 'I thought I heard you moving about,' she said, smothering a yawn. 'Couldn't you sleep?'

'I've been out to buy the papers.' Dee pushed the still folded favourite at her. 'Here, take it back to bed and read it with your tea.'

But Claire had spotted the other paper lying on the chair where it had fallen. Bobby's smiling face uppermost. She picked it up. 'What made you buy this rag?' she asked.

Dee shrugged. 'Need you ask? Look at the front page—then at the centre spread.'

Claire did as she was told, took one look and sighed. 'There was something similar in the local paper yesterday. I put it away out of sight.'

Dee poured the tea. 'You should have known I'd find out sooner or later. It doesn't bother me. One look at that headline tells you how how wrong they can get things!'

Claire was turning the pages. 'There's quite a bit about Greig Meredith here too,' she said. 'They've raked up all they could lay hands on about him too, it seems.' She passed the paper to Dee, who shook her head, glancing at the clock.

'Haven't time to read it now. I'd better get myself some breakfast and get across to the hospital. Bobby's due in theatre at nine-thirty.'

Claire looked surprised. 'He'll be woozy from his pre-med by the time you get there. Still, no doubt he'll be glad to see you before they take him down.'

'I'm observing,' Dee told her briefly, pouring corn-flakes into a bowl and fetching milk from the fridge.

Claire stared at her. 'Is that wise?'

'Don't *you* start!' Dee looked up at her friend. 'I wanted to swap pláces with Janet Hall and scrub for it, but Greig wouldn't allow it.'

'I should just think not!'

'I told him I wouldn't let it get to me, but he was adamant.'

Claire kept her thoughts to herself. It was Dee's business, but in her opinion the other girl was carrying loyalty a little too far.

When she looked into his room fifteen minutes later, Dee found Bobby drowsy from the pre-med injection as Claire had predicted. She sat with him for a while, but he kept drifting off in the middle of a sentence and in the end she stood up, whispered 'Good luck' and tiptoed out of the room to take the lift down to the surgical unit.

The viewing room was crowded. Most of the medical students plus quite a large number of housemen had turned up to watch Bobby's operation. When Dee walked in she felt as though all eyes were upon her. Most of the people present knew of the connection between her and Bobby and no one questioned her right to be there. Silently they moved up to make room for her on the front row of seats that faced the bank of closed circuit television screens. She found herself sitting between two fourth-year medical students, one of whom had asked her out several times. He smiled hesitantly at her and cleared his throat.

'Bad luck about Carr's crash,' he ventured. 'I'm sure he'll be okay though. Meredith's a wizard at this kind of thing.'

She smiled back. 'I know.'

After a pause he spoke again: 'I bet you've forgotten me. I'm Bill Kenlaw.'

'I hadn't forgotten. How are you?'

'I'm fine, thanks.' He pulled a tightly folded newspaper out of his pocket and glanced at her sideways. 'I—er——Have you seen this morning's paper?'

Glancing sideways at the paper in his hands, she saw

that it was the same one she had bought earlier, the one with the feature about Bobby. 'Yes, thanks,' she told him shortly.

He reddened and put it away again. 'I—just didn't want it to come as a shock.'

She turned to him. 'If you believe everything you read in that kind of newspaper, you'll be disappointed not to be watching an amputation this morning!'

Bill looked startled for a moment, then grinned. 'Okay—point taken.'

Something was happening now in the operating theatre. Nurse Hall had everything ready and the patient was being wheeled in. The anaesthetist took up his position; Greig and his team entered and he began to speak. A hush descended on the occupants of the viewing room as everyone present prepared to settle down and concentrate.

With the help of the X-ray photographs Greig pointed out the extent of Bobby's injuries to those assisting him, as well as the watchers in the viewing room. He spoke about the patient's excellent physical condition and the type of anaesthetic to be used. He estimated the time he expected to take on the operation and outlined exactly what he intended to do. Then he set to work. Beginning with the right leg and making a Mercedes incision, he screwed a wafer-thin stainless steel plate to the knee joint and to the sound part of the tibia, almost halfway down, explaining as he did so that this was more to help him to locate the shattered bone than to reinforce it. As he worked, the silence in the viewing room was almost tangible. In her fascination at the surgeon's skill, Dee even forgot that the man undergoing this delicate operation was Bobby. Fragment by fragment, the shattered bone was fitted together like pieces in a living jigsaw puzzle until at last work on the right leg was completed and ready for suturing. In close-ups Dee could see the beads of perspiration on Greig's brow, blotted occasionally by the Theatre Sister as he worked, and at the end of suturing he announced that he would be taking a brief break to snatch a cup of coffee, re-scrub and change his surgical gloves.

His estimation of the time was fairly accurate. By the time he had completed the work on both Bobby's legs and hands it would be all of eight hours since he had begun. Bill Kenlaw slipped out at one o'clock while Greig was taking the first of his breaks. When he slid back into his seat he passed Dee a packet of sandwiches and a plastic beaker of coffee. She looked up at him in surprise. 'Oh—thanks, Bill.'

He grinned at her. 'I thought it was time you had a break too,' he said. 'You've been staring unblinkingly at those screens for hours. Can't have you expiring with hunger, can we?'

She ate the sandwiches and drank the coffee grate-fully. Bill was right, she wouldn't have dared leave her seat for fear of missing some vital detail of the operation.

When Bobby was finally wheeled into the recovery room it was just after five o'clock. Many of the students had already left, and when Dee got to her feet she found that she was stiff, both with sitting still for so long and with the tension of concentrating. Her eyes felt sore and gritty too. Bill looked at her.

'Brilliant, wasn't it?'

She nodded. 'Fantastic.'

He hesitated. 'What are you going to do now?'

She shrugged. 'Go home for a bath and something to eat. Later I hope to slip in and take a peep at Bobby.'

'You wouldn't like to have a bite to eat with me first, I suppose?'

'Sorry, Bill. It's really kind of you to ask, but I'm sure you understand. I have to be around.'

He looked at her for a long moment as though

wondering whether to say what was in his mind, then he shrugged and smiled at her. 'Okay. Maybe some other time. 'Bye.'

'Goodbye, Bill.'

As she walked out into the fresh air Dee was filled with a feeling of anticlimax. She told herself she should be glad—for Bobby and for Greig. The operation had seemed so successful. The prognosis couldn't be better. But it had been all too clear what was in Bill's mind. No doubt it was in the minds of a good many other people too, especially those who had seen this morning's papers. Maybe they'd be thinking that she wasn't the only girl who would 'be around' to help Bobby's recovery.

Greig sat in the little office next to Theatre Four staring down at the report he had just completed. As far as he could tell at this stage, the operation had been a complete success. His colleagues had congratulated him warmly in the changing room afterwards and he knew himself that he had done his finest work. If Bobby Carr was as determined as he gave every indication of being he would be walking normally again within a year at the outside. And no doubt also within that time he would be risking his life again on the racing track. Well, that was his business. Unfortunately it would be Dee's as well. Greig sighed and flexed his shoulders. He felt stiff and tired, longing for nothing more than a long hot bath and an hour's relaxation. He thought of Dee and wondered if she had been in the viewing room. Somehow he felt sure she had been. The thought both comforted and depressed him at the same time.

Because of the long hours Bobby had spent under surgery he went straight from the theatre back into Intensive Care and was allowed no visitors that evening.

Greig went to check him at ten o'clock and found him conscious and quite cheerful—wanting to know when he could go back to his own room and start working towards a full recovery. So far, of course, he was feeling little pain. Tomorrow would be the real test, but Greig decided not to warn him.

'Just try to get a good night's sleep,' he said. 'We'll talk about that in the morning.'

Dee had gone straight to bed after a snatched meal and had fallen asleep almost at once, walking only when the alarm shrilled at six-thirty the following morning. She was back on the early shift this morning and she was glad to be finished by lunchtime. Hurrying home, she changed and made herself a quick sandwich, then hurried across to the hospital again, buying a paperback thriller and a box of Bobby's favourite sweets on her way. Claire had told her that he had been allowed back to his private room again after Greig had seen him during the morning, so she went straight to the private wing.

The young nurse on the desk was one Dee had never seen before, and when she asked for Bobby the girl shook her head.

'Oh, I'm sorry, but he's only allowed one visitor at a time, and his girl-friend is with him now.' She leaned forward confidentially. 'She's come all the way down from London this afternoon, just to see him. She's a model, you know. Her pictures's been in all the papers.' She sighed gustily. 'It's *ever* so romantic!'

With a rueful smile Dee handed over the book and sweets. 'Maybe you'll give him these, in that case.'

The girl looked apologetic. 'Oh, what a shame. Maybe you could come back later. Who shall I say was asking?'

It was on the tip of Dee's tongue to tell the girl she was

Bobby's fiancée, just to see the look on her face. But she stopped herself, simply giving her name; partly because it would have been unkind and partly because, almost without realising it, she no longer thought of herself as Bobby's fiancée. In fact she hardly even felt any resentment at Geraldine's name being linked with Bobby's or the publicity she had received. She was mulling over the significance of this in her mind as she walked along the corridor and pressed the lift button, so deep in thought that until his voice broke into her thoughts she didn't even notice Greig walk up quietly to join her.

'A penny for them,' he offered. 'Though they look as though they're worth a great deal more!'

Dee turned and her face brightened. 'Oh, hello.'

'Been visiting Bobby?'

She shook her head. 'That *was* the idea, but someone else got there before me.'

He inclined his head. 'Really—who?'

'I was told his girl-friend was with him.' She mimicked the young nurse's dreamy tones: 'She's come *all* the way from London specially to see him. It's *ever* so romantic!'

Greig smiled, recognising Dee's imitation. 'Ah, that would be little Nurse Freeman. Not exactly the soul of tact. I'll get Sister to have a word with her.'

'Oh no! She only spoke the truth,' said Dee. 'By the way, congratulations. The operation was fascinating. Everyone's talking about it this morning.'

'You were there, then?'

'Of course. I wouldn't have missed it for anything.'

Greig regarded her for a moment, wondering if she would have watched him work for eight hours if the patient been unknown to her.

'How is he doing?' she asked him.

'Of course, you haven't seen him. He's progressing very well indeed,' Greig told her. 'He's even made a start on exercising his calf muscles.' He sighed. 'I have to hand it to him—he's got guts. The pain must be excruciating, but you know how much determination he has.'

The lift arrived and the doors opened. Greig glanced at her as they stepped inside. 'Are you doing anything at the moment?'

She shrugged. 'Under the circumstances, no.'

'Come and have a cup of tea with me. There must be questions you'd like to ask.'

She looked doubtful. 'Are you sure? Aren't you busy?'

He patted his top pocket. 'If I'm needed they'll bleep me. I think the flat might be the quietest place. What do you think?'

As they sat over cups of tea in Greig's living room, he studied Dee's face. He had vowed faithfully to keep out of her way, but she had looked so tired and strained when he saw her waiting for the lift that his heart had twisted. Even now he was fighting down an urge to reach for her hand.

'Bobby's legs will be fine,' he told her. 'He should be trying them out before too long and walking normally again in a few months. He did lose the top joint of his left index finger, though.'

Dee smiled. 'I'm sure he'll cope with that!'

There was a silence as he looked at her. 'The girl-friend—I take it that was the girl in the papers—the model, Geraldine something or other?' She nodded and he went on: 'The same girl he was at the cinema with that evening.' He bit his tongue. Damn! That sounded like rubbing it in.

She looked up at him quickly. 'Yes, that's right, Geraldine Moore.' Anxious to change the subject, she asked: 'I suppose you haven't had second thoughts about the house?'

Greig shook his head. 'I've hardly had time to think of anything but work. As you said, it would be fun to do it up, but it's out of the question as far as I'm concerned. It's cheap enough as it stands, but all the improvements would cost a bomb. Besides, it's really a family house.'

Dee sighed. 'I suppose you're right. I fell in love with it at first sight, though, didn't you?' For some reason he seemed preoccupied and she leaned forward. 'Didn't you?'

He looked up from stirring his tea abstractedly. 'Sorry —didn't I what?'

'Fall in love at first sight,' she repeated. Their eyes met and she felt her cheeks colouring. 'W-with the house, I mean,' she added falteringly.

Greig's hand inched towards hers till their fingertips touched. His eyes still holding hers, he asked quietly: 'I promised myself I wouldn't ask you, Dee, but you've had time to think about it now. Are you really going through with it? Will you still marry Carr—put up with that frenetic lifestyle, the risks, the uncertainty?'

She swallowed hard, trying to drag her eyes away from his compelling golden stare. 'I have to if—if he still wants me to.'

'After making up your mind to end it—writing that letter?' He leaned towards her, his eyes searching hers relentlessly. 'You realise it'll mean giving up your own career, don't you? Everything you've worked for— everything that's important to you? Do you *really* love him enough to make that kind of sacrifice?' His eyes searched hers. '*Do* you, Dee?'

'He could have died,' she told him, avoiding the penetrating eyes. 'Or worse. If his operation hadn't been successful—if you hadn't given him back his chance to race again, I dread to think what might have become of him.'

His eyes widened. 'Are you telling me *I've* given him back to you?'

Very gently she withdrew her hand from his. 'It matters so much to him, Greig. I ought to have seen that when I made him promise to give it up. Now that he has this second chance, almost—well, almost *in spite* of me, I can't do any other than keep my promise.'

Greig caught at her hand again, gripping her fingers tightly this time, his eyes holding hers compellingly as he said: 'You're not answering my questions. *Do you love him enough to make that kind of sacrifice?*'

Dee felt the tears constrict her throat into a painful knot. It wasn't fair! Why was he pushing her into a corner, tormenting her like this? 'Why should *you* care?' she flung at him with a sudden shrillness that shocked him. 'What do you get out of baiting me like this? Can't you see that I'm trying to do the right thing? Why the hell can't you leave me alone?' She bit her lip hard and instantly felt the hot tears welling up. 'Oh, God!—I'm sorry,' she muttered, snatching her hand away to fumble for a handkerchief. 'I shouldn't have said that.' She rose uncertainly to her feet. 'I'd better go, before I make a complete idiot of myself.' Without a backward glance she fled from the flat and up the stairs to the top flat. It was only then that she realised that she had left her handbag, with her key inside it, in Greig's flat. Leaning helplessly against the door, she felt all the strength drain from her as the tears overflowed to slide down her cheeks.

'You'll be needing this.' He spoke quietly, holding out the bag to her. She turned a stricken, tear-stained face towards him and the next second she was in his arms, crying against his shoulder while he held her close. He sighed and closed his eyes. There was so much he wanted to say to her, so much advice he wanted to give her, but he knew now that he was too hopelessly involved to be able to give it objectively. Anything he had to say now would only be making life even harder for both of them. She must work it out for herself or not at all, however hard it would be to stand by and watch. Greig had spoken to her of sacrifice, but he wondered if she would ever know just how much of that sacrifice was his. A feeling of aching longing, of near-despair, swept devastatingly through him as he stood there holding her trembling body in his arms. She was about to throw herself—and all his dreams—away like so much rubbish, and there was nothing he could do but stand on the sidelines and watch like a passive spectator.

When Dee returned to the hospital an hour later Bobby was alone. She found him propped up in bed, looking tired and cross. He greeted her with: 'Oh, so you finally decided to come and see if I was still alive!'

Dee found a chair and sat down. 'I did come earlier,' she told him. 'But Geraldine was here, and you're only allowed one visitor at a time.'

He groaned. 'Oh God, don't tell me you're going to start all that again!'

'No, Bobby. Obviously your friends will want to come and visit,' she told him calmly. 'It was good of Geraldine to come all the way from London.'

'She'd have come before, but she had a modelling assignment over the weekend,' he told her, a touch of pride in his voice. 'And guess what—she reckons she can talk her old man into sponsoring me when I'm back in the racing game again. As long as I don't take too long about it my name'll be a big draw now, you know.'

'Yes, I dare say you're right.' Anxious to change the subject, Dee asked him how he felt, but he seemed uncommunicative about his condition. She told herself that it was only to be expected after what he had been through. 'I watched your operation from the viewing room yesterday,' she told him. 'It was . . .' She broke off. He was staring at her with an expression of undisguised horror.

'You were watching?'

'Yes. It was a wonderful operation, Bobby. You're lucky to have had such a brilliant surgeon . . .'

'God!' he exploded. 'You might at least have spared me that!'

She shook her head perplexedly. 'But I'm a nurse, Bobby. It was the nearest I could get to . . .'

'Don't!' he broke in, shaking his head. 'Surely you could have considered my feelings. How do you expect me to react?' The very idea of her seeing him on the operating table, being carved up like a lump of meat on a butcher's slab, was utterly repulsive to him.

Dee was at a loss for a moment, then she said: 'I hear you've been exercising. That's good.'

'I suppose you all discuss me like some interesting medical programme you've seen on the telly,' he snapped. 'Yes, I've been exercising, and you wouldn't think it was good if *you* had to do it. It's agony!'

She touched his arm. 'You look tired. It's early days. Perhaps you've been trying to do too much. There's always tomorrow, you know.'

'Yes! Always tomorrow—and the next day and the day after *that*!' He flung at her bitterly. 'In other words, it's going to be a bloody long job. There's no need to rub that in too!'

'I'm not, Bobby.' Dee was silent. It was natural for Bobby to be depressed and irritable, but she couldn't help wondering . . . 'Have you remembered anything about last Friday?' she asked.

He shook his head. 'No, but it doesn't matter any more. All I'm bothered about now is *next* Friday. It's the future that matters now.'

She touched his shoulder. 'If it's any help, I'll be here,' she told him.

He turned to look at her, his expression relaxing a little. 'Sorry, kid, I know you're trying to cheer me up. I'm in a foul mood. Maybe you were right; maybe I should rest for a while.'

She stood up, suddenly realising with a stab of shame that she was relieved at the chance to escape. 'I—I'll go, then.'

Bobby nodded. 'Okay—see you. Oh, thanks for the book and the sweets.'

As she walked down the corridor Dee thought of Greig's words: *You realise you'll have to give up your own career—everything you've worked for? Do you really love him enough to make that sacrifice?* She bit her lip, refusing to listen to the answer that lay deep in her heart.

Alone, Bobby relaxed against the pillows. He felt deathly tired. Closing his eyes, he thought about the two visitors he had had this afternoon; of Geraldine, so vivacious; her lovely face so full of life and her conversation bubbling over with news of her own blossoming career. It had done him good to hear about it; made him forget his own troubles for half an hour. Then there was Dee. He winced. She'd actually watched them operating on him! He couldn't get over it. How could anyone, let alone a pretty, feminine girl like Dee, want—actually *want*—to see something like that? The knowledge of her having been there made him feel lowered—emasculated. He opened his eyes with a renewed rush of strength. He *had* to get back to normal again, get the use back into his legs as soon as possible. The idea of being helpless, at the mercy of others, was utterly terrifying to him. Gritting his teeth, he began again—bending his toes upwards towards him as far as he could, just as the physio had shown him this morning. He took a deep breath and then pressed them back again towards the bed. Even the agonising pain that racked his calf muscles brought him a certain relief. While he was concentrating on that he wasn't feeling anything else.

Claire was out for the evening and Dee sat alone in the flat, staring unseeingly at the flickering television screen. Her conversation with Bobby had dismayed her more than words could tell. She was a nurse, yet she had felt totally at a loss. She hadn't known what to say to him and when she had spoken she had said the wrong thing and upset him. If she couldn't handle the situation now, when he was ill, how could she cope when he was back on his feet again and determined to pick up where he had left off? Inevitably there would be snags and setbacks. He would feel angry and frustrated with himself at first. Maybe Greig was right when he said that she was making too great a sacrifice? She sighed. He would never know just how great that sacrifice was—that she had only discovered when it was too late what falling in love really meant.

When the telephone rang she started, switching on the table lamp; blinking as the sudden flood of light filled the corners of the darkening room. She got to her feet and went into the kitchen to answer it.

'Hello, Deanne Latimer speaking.'

'Deanne. It's me, Lena Carr. May I come and see you, dear?'

Dee was slightly taken aback. 'Well—yes, of course.'

'Are you alone?'

'Yes, my flatmate is out for the evening. Is anything wrong?' Dee couldn't imagine Lena Carr wanting to see her for purely social reasons.

The older woman laughed. 'Good heavens, no! I'd just like a chat, that's all. Look, I've been to see Bobby and I'm at the hospital, so I'll be with you in about five minutes, if that's all right.'

'Of course—I'll put the coffee on.'

Dee replaced the receiver and stood chewing her lip thoughtfully. Lena's honeyed tones were a vast contrast to her hostile attitude the last time they had met. What could she want? She had just had time to start the coffee-maker and set out the cups when there was a ring at the doorbell, and she answered it to find Lena standing outside. In the living room she took off her coat and handed it to Dee, who indicated one of the armchairs.

'Do make yourself at home,' she invited. 'I'll just get the coffee. It's almost ready.'

Still puzzled as to the reason for Bobby's mother's visit, she carried the tray into the living room and poured the coffee. Lena watched her thoughtfully, took a sip of her coffee and then put the cup down on the table in front of her.

'Bobby seemed quite bright under the circumstances, I thought,' she remarked. 'What did you think of him?'

Dee nodded. 'As you say, he's doing well.'

'Of course I understand that we must keep his morale up,' Lena went on. 'But we all know that he's going to be disabled when he leaves hospital. I don't think there's any denying that, is there?'

'Oh, not at all—but Mr Meredith says . . .'

Lena was shaking her head. 'I'm really quite surprised at a man like him,' she said. 'Encouraging a patient to go out and undo all the work he put into him.' She shook her head. 'Except that of course he knows it will never happen. But that's not what I came to say.' Dee waited, at a complete loss to understand the reason for Lena's sudden change of attitude. 'I may as well be completely honest with you, my dear. I haven't always approved of Bobby's relationship with you,' Lena went on. 'Oh, for no other reason than that you seemed so utterly unsuited to each other,' she added hurriedly. 'But now of course things have changed quite drastically. I think you're quite probably exactly the right person for him now that this has happened. I know he's always been very fond of you and . . .'

Dee swallowed uneasily. 'What are you trying to say, Mrs Carr?' she asked bluntly.

The smile dissolved from Lena's face as she opened her handbag and drew out an envelope. 'This came for Bobby after he'd left for the race track on Friday morning,' she said. 'He asked for his mail to be brought in to him today, but his father and I agreed that it wouldn't be wise for him to receive anything that would excite or depress him. In order to avoid this I opened the few letters that had arrived. This was among them.' She passed the single sheet of paper to Dee, but there was no need for her to read it; she knew its contents all too well. 'I thought you might want to tear it up under the circumstances,' Lena said pointedly. 'I haven't mentioned it to anyone else, not even George. I felt so certain that you'd written it on impulse.' She smiled again. 'You'll thank me, of course. I know the last thing you'd want would be to deliver a blow like this to Bobby after what's happened.'

CHAPTER TEN

DEE met the eyes of the older woman sitting opposite her. Lena Carr seemed to be waiting for an explanation.

'As you've read the letter I wrote to Bobby I may as well tell you that it wasn't written on impulse,' she said slowly. 'You were right—Bobby and I are unsuited to each other. Lately I'd realised that. I felt it was time to end our relationship.'

'Couldn't you have told him so face to face?' Lena asked coldly.

'I meant to—after the race,' Dee told her. 'I never meant to post that letter. It was only written to clarify my feelings. Somehow I dropped it, and someone must have picked it up and put it in the post for me.' Even to her own ears it sounded like a feeble excuse, but it was the truth and she could offer no other explanation. She shrugged. 'That's the truth, Mrs Carr. I didn't want to upset Bobby before the race—it meant too much to him.'

'But you persuaded him to give up his racing,' Lena reminded her. 'You were the only person who ever managed to do that. That's why . . .' she broke off, and suddenly everything was clear to Dee. Lena wanted her to marry Bobby now. As a nurse she would be able to take care of him—because Lena still believed he would be crippled. But she was hedging her bets. If by some miraculous chance he should ever be fit to take up racing again, Dee was the one person capable of dissuading him. As for Lena's feelings about Geraldine's suitability as a daughter-in-law—those would have quickly vanished when Bobby disclosed the fact that her father would sponsor him once he was fit to race again.

Dee rose to her feet. 'I think we're forgetting one thing, Mrs Carr,' she said steadily. 'Bobby will make the final choice, whatever plans anyone makes for him.' She looked the older woman in the eye. 'There's nothing wrong with his brain. He's still capable of making his own decisions.'

Lena's face drained of colour as she rose to face Dee. She was several inches taller and seemed to tower over her as she said: 'So far the papers have left you alone, Deanne. That must have been a great relief to you.' Her eyes narrowed. 'I wonder what they'd make of a nurse who broke off her engagement when her fiancé lay badly injured in hospital—the same hospital where she herself worked! I should think they'd have a field day, wouldn't you?' Her eyes glinted with triumph as she looked down at Dee. 'It wouldn't do much for the noble, *angelic* image, would it?' She bent and snatched up the letter from the coffee table where Dee had put it. 'I'm sure they'd be fascinated to see the letter breaking the engagement—received on the morning of the race!'

Her heart beating unevenly, Dee whispered: 'Are you trying to blackmail me, Mrs Carr?'

But the word left Lena unruffled. 'Don't be melodramatic, dear. I'm just trying to help you to see things more clearly. We've all been through a very trying time, and one tends to get over-emotional.' She smiled. 'And please call me Lena,' she said sweetly. 'After all, we'll be related soon, won't we?' She gathered up her things and cast a steely eye over Dee. 'I'll leave you now. I'm sure you have a lot to think about.'

When she had gone reaction overtook Dee. She found herself shaking from head to foot. The revelation that Bobby had never actually received her letter was, on the face of it, a tremendous relief. It told her that she could not have been the cause of his accident. She could break with him now without feeling guilty. On the other hand, if she did, and Lena carried out her threat to show her letter to the press . . . She shuddered at the thought of the publicity. It could mean suspension—even resigning her job here at Queen Eleanor's. Suddenly the walls of the flat seemed to close in on her; she desperately wanted company, someone she could talk to, and without even consciously thinking about it, she found herself on her way down the stairs.

During the evening she had lost all track of time, and it was only when there was no response to her tapping on Greig's door that she looked at her watch and found to her surprise that it was after eleven o'clock. She was just turning away when she heard a movement inside the flat, and a moment later the door opened and Greig looked out.

'Dee! Is something wrong?' He wore a bathrobe and his hair was damp and ruffled.

She shook her head. 'No—it's all right. I didn't realise it was so late. Please go back to bed. I'll . . .'

She broke off as he grasped her arm and pulled her inside the flat. 'Don't run away, silly! I wasn't in bed, I was in the bath.' He looked down at her, his eyes troubled. 'What's happened? You look like death.'

'I—er . . .' She swallowed, suddenly at a loss. Where did one begin? The whole thing had become convoluted —coiled inside her head like a spring about to snap. 'Oh, Greig, Mrs Carr has just been to see me—there's been a—a development,' she lifted her shoulders helplessly. 'I—don't know what to do!'

Taking her by the elbows, he eased her into a chair, then went to pour her a brandy. Placing the glass firmly into her hand, he commanded: 'Drink that. I'll be back in a minute. Then I want to hear about this *development, all* of it, from the beginning—right?'

When he returned a few minutes later, having hastily

donned a pair of jeans and a sweater, he found her calmer. Slowly she recounted the conversation with Lena Carr and the ultimatum the other woman had handed her. Somehow, even the telling of it took the heat out of the situation and made it appear slightly less bizarre. Greig's calm presence had a soothing effect on her. Sitting opposite her, leaning forward, his elbows on his knees, he listened attentively without comment until Dee had finally finished her story. She looked up at him, suddenly aware of the imposition of calling on him at this time of night and pouring out problems that were no concern of his.

'Thanks for listening, Greig,' she said, getting to her feet. 'I shouldn't have bothered you with all this. I'm not expecting you to become involved in it—it was just that I desperately needed to talk to someone.' She summoned a smile. 'Thanks for the brandy. I feel much better now. I'll go and let you get your sleep.'

He sprang up, reaching out a hand to stop her. 'Wait a minute! Sit down. Why do you say you shouldn't have bothered me with it?'

She stared up at him. 'Well, because—it's not your problem, is it?'

He looked down into her eyes, his hands resting on her shoulders. '*Isn't* it, Dee?'

His eyes held hers and she felt her heart stir. Those three words told her that she was not alone—and suggested more, much more, though she hardly dared to let the feeling jell.

Greig gently pressed her back into the corner of the settee and sat beside her, taking her hand firmly in both of his. 'Before you leave here we have to work something out,' he told her earnestly. 'You can't go to bed with all this on your mind.' She nodded, sighing deeply at the sheer relief of having someone with whom to share her worry. 'You're quite wrong when you say this isn't my problem, Dee,' he went on. 'What you've just told me naturally concerns me. Bobby Carr is my patient, after all.'

His patient! Dee looked at him, trying hard to fight down a feeling of disappointment. 'Oh, yes—yes, of course,' she whispered. 'And you've no need to worry; I shan't do anything to jeopardise his recovery.'

Greig grasped both her shoulders and pulled her round to face him. 'Dee, listen to me. I want some straight answers from you,' he commanded. 'No more hedging. Just how deep are your feelings for Bobby? If you really love him I'm sure you've nothing here you can't work out. If you don't, then you need advice.'

He bent his head slightly to look into her lowered eyes, and suddenly she knew the meaning of the phrase, 'the moment of truth'. Her voice was little more than a whisper and her head was still lowered as she said: 'You were right—nothing has changed. What I feel for Bobby is no more love than it was then. I don't think I truly knew what love was . . .' She only just stopped herself from adding *'till now.'* She looked up at him, her eyes meeting his. 'But I think you knew that even before I did, didn't you, Greig?'

'Yes, I think I did.' For a moment it was as though time was suspended. Greig had the curious feeling that the words she had spoken hung in the air like frozen crystals. He wanted to reach out and grasp them—to keep and cherish them. The relief in his heart was almost overwhelming, but his voice betrayed none of this as he said calmly: 'I think that the sooner you tell him—the sooner you put your feelings on the line, the better.'

'But he's so vulnerable just now. How can I? It would look so heartless. And what if his mother goes ahead and carries out her threat?'

His fingers tightened on her shoulders as he shook her slightly. 'Dee, listen, let's get all this into perspective. In my opinion Mrs Carr is bluffing. I know she's an unpleasant woman, but try to see her view of things. Bobby is her son and she loves him. Racing almost took him from her, and naturally that frightened her. At the moment she'd do anything to keep him out of it.'

He released his grip on her shoulders as he felt her relax a little. 'Now, to begin with—that letter is not her property. It's addressed to Bobby and she would have to have his permission to disclose it to the press. Somehow I don't think he'd give it. If I've read him right, public sympathy is about the last thing he'd want to invite, and who would know that better than his mother? Secondly, the media have never even *heard* of you! They have Geraldine Moore down as the girl in Bobby's life. Frankly I don't think they'd be very interested in the story.'

Dee's eyes widened with relief. 'I hadn't thought of it that way.'

'I suggest that you forget about the press for the time being and take one thing at a time,' he told her. 'Bobby is your first priority. Go and see him tomorrow, tell him how you feel. Put your cards on the table and talk things through.'

'You—don't think that would be too upsetting under the circumstances?'

Greig shook his head. 'Put it this way, what his mother is planning would be far more upsetting for all concerned in the long run.' He felt the tension go out of her shoulders. Under his hands she felt so small and fragile. He wanted to gather her into his arms, to tell her he would always take care of her—that he loved her. But he held himself firmly in check. She must break with Bobby Carr first. He must not complicate life still further for her. With one finger he gently tipped up her chin to look enquiringly into her eyes. 'Feeling happier now?'

She nodded, smiling. 'Much, thank you. Though I'll be glad when I've talked to Bobby.'

'Of course.' He stood up and pulled her to her feet. 'Now off you go and get some sleep.'

She stood looking up at him, longing for the comfort of his arms around her. 'Will I see you tomorrow?' she asked.

He nodded. 'If you want to. You know where I am. Tomorrow is my day off, so I'll be here all day. I have some letters and some paperwork to catch up on.' Cupping her chin, he bent and brushed her forehead with his lips, fighting down the desire to crush her in his arms. 'Try not to worry,' he told her huskily. 'Everything will be all right—I guarantee it!'

To her surprise Dee slept well and woke refreshed. She had decided not to tell Claire about Lena Carr's visit. She would tell no one, not even Bobby, unless she were forced. After all, thinking about it, she doubted very much whether Lena herself would be anxious to confide her devious plotting to anyone.

In Theatre One Sister Fairchild was back, looking rested and refreshed after her holiday. As they prepared the theatre she told Dee about her stay in Edinburgh and how much she had enjoyed it.

'By the way,' she remarked, 'just before I went away I found a letter of yours on the floor of the rest room. It must have escaped your notice when you dropped your handbag. I posted it for you. Was that all right?'

Dee sighed. If she only knew! 'Yes, that was all right. Thank you, Sister.'

There was no one who knew the work of the emergency theatre quite like Sister Fairchild, and the morning shift went smoothly. Even Mr Thurman remarked that he had missed her, which brought a blush of pleasure to her cheeks.

The shift over, Dee went back to the flat for a quick snack and to change out of her uniform. Every time she thought of what she had to do this afternoon her stomach lurched with apprehension, and when she had prepared the bowl of soup and the ham sandwich, all she could do was pick at it uninterestedly. Finally she pushed the tray away from her and rose deliberately to her feet. It was now or never. Better get it over with.

When she arrived on the private wing Dee found Nurse Freeman once again on duty at the reception desk. The girl looked up with a smile.

'Oh, hello! You're in luck today. Mr Carr has no visitors at the moment. He had a long session with the physio this morning and he's been working hard at his exercises ever since. Sister had to insist on his taking a rest.' She giggled. 'He's probably bored by now, so he'll be glad to see you.'

Dee hid a smile. Greig had been right. Little Nurse Freeman had a lot to learn where tact and diplomacy were concerned. 'Thanks,' she said. 'I'll try not to tire him.'

Nurse Freeman waved a hand airily. 'Oh, don't worry, stay as long as you like. His girl-friend isn't coming in until this evening.'

As Dee entered the room Bobby looked up with a smile. 'Hi! I wondered if you'd look in. I'm sorry about last night, Dee. I was in a foul mood.'

She drew up a chair to his bedside, her heart quickening. 'It's all right, Bobby, I do understand. How are you feeling? How's the physio going?'

'Great.' He winced. 'Well, no, not all that great, if I'm truthful,' he confessed. 'They won't let me do as much as I'd like and what little I do hurts like crazy. But I can't give up. I've made up my mind to be out of here within the month.'

Dee was silent. Now that she was actually here her

nerve was running out on her. He was trying so hard to get on his feet again. His courage and determination had amazed everyone. How *could* she say what she had come here to say under the circumstances?

'Anything up?' he asked, peering at her. 'You're looking a bit down.'

She shook her head, trying to smile. 'No, I'm fine. A bit tired, maybe. We had a busy shift . . .' She trailed off—her excuses sounded lame, even to her. She racked her mind for some way to begin what she had to say, for some gentle way to drop her bombshell.

Bobby was watching her unobserved, puzzled about her nervousness, which, if the truth were known, matched his own. He took a deep breath, but when he spoke it was at the same time as her:

'Look, Dee . . .'

'Bobby, I . . .'

They both laughed and he prompted: 'Sorry. Go on.'

'No—you first.'

He frowned. 'It's just—look, Dee, there's something I have to say. It isn't easy and I don't know quite how to begin.' He turned to look at her. 'Dee—since this prang of mine everything's changed. Somehow things look different. I know I promised you I'd give it up, but now I know I can't. I just *have* to get back!'

'I should never have asked you to give up . . .' she began.

But he shook his head, frowning. 'No, Dee, don't interrupt. This is damned difficult, and if I don't say it in one go I might never find the bottle again.' He sighed. 'I know it's on the cards that I might be back in hospital a few more times before I'm finished; it's what you might call an occupational hazard. I know you're a nurse and—and used to these things . . .' He shook his head impatiently. 'Look, what I'm trying to say is this: having you see me like that, out cold on the operating table—all carved up . . .' he shook his head, 'makes me feel—well, *odd* about us.'

She had been wondering just what he was trying to say, but suddenly light dawned. Bobby's masculine image had been badly bruised by the knowledge that she had seen him at his most vulnerable. Unlike his physical injuries it was something that couldn't be healed. 'Are you saying you want to end our relationship, Bobby?' she asked gently.

His eyes avoided hers. 'I guess that *is* what I'm trying to say, yes.'

'I understand,' she assured him. 'I expect a lot of men would probably feel the same. The romance has been killed for you—because of me working in the theatre.'

'Why couldn't I have put it so neatly?' He gave her a rueful grin. 'You always hated racing, didn't you, Dee? I always felt I'd pushed you into agreeing to get engaged. Maybe this won't be too much of a blow to you, eh?'

She smiled, relief flooding through her. Now she needn't tell him. She could leave him with his ego intact. She knew Bobby well enough to know that was vitally important to him. 'It's true that I've never really felt that I was right for you,' she told him gently. 'There were lots of areas we didn't see eye to eye on and probably never would have done.' She looked at him. 'If you really want to know, I think Geraldine is far more your type. She'll enjoy being there to watch you race, cheering you on. And that's what you want, isn't it?'

He smiled gratefully at her. 'So you're not hurt, then, Dee?' he asked. 'I've been worrying about that. I never wanted—never *meant* to hurt you, you know.'

She shook her head. 'No, Bobby, I'm not hurt. Don't worry any more.'

'Honestly?' he searched her eyes.

'Honestly.'

He regarded her gravely. 'You deserve someone

better than me,' he told her. 'Some doctor, maybe. Someone like Meredith—all upright and dedicated.' He chuckled. 'He doesn't approve of me at all, you know.'

'Try to see it his way,' she said quickly. 'How would you feel if you'd put in a lot of work on a bike and then someone took it out and smashed it up again?'

He shot her a swift look. 'But that's what I do all the time! Setting things up to knock them down. That's my life, see what I mean?'

Dee smiled and shook her head at him. He was right: never in a dozen lifetimes would they ever see things in the same light. She stood up and dropped a kiss on his forehead. 'You need to rest, Bobby, so I'm going now. I'll look in from time to time to see how you're coming along. Take care of yourself.'

'You too, kid. And—good luck!'

At the door she paused, looking back at him. 'One piece of advice, Bobby. If you're going to ask Geraldine to marry you, I'd do it soon before someone else snaps her up.'

He grinned back at her. 'Don't worry—that's one department I don't need physio for!'

Standing on the hospital steps, Dee drew in a deep breath of the warm air. Suddenly it tasted like champagne for her. For the first time in months she felt free, and there was only one person she wanted to share the feeling with.

When he opened his door in response to her knock she could see that Greig had been working. His desk was littered with papers and the remains of a hurriedly snatched lunch, and she noticed that there were tiny lines of strain around his eyes.

'Come in.' He held the door open for her to come inside, looking at her enquiringly.

'I've just come from the hospital,' she told him. 'From visiting Bobby.'

He raised an eyebrow. 'And . . . ?'

'Before I could begin what I wanted to tell him, Bobby had something important he wanted to say to me,' she told him. 'It was that he felt our relationship had run its course. In other words, it's over—with no emotion or hard words. No tears or bad feeling.'

His features softened into a smile. 'So all that agonising was for nothing?'

Dee smiled. 'Yes. The feeling was mutual.' She didn't quite know what reaction she had expected, but as they stood looking at each other it was as though a barrier had suddenly descended between them. Suddenly she felt in the way. Puzzled, she took an involuntary step backwards. 'Well, I thought I'd let you know.' She nodded in the direction of the littered desk. 'I can see you're busy. I won't keep you any longer.'

'No. Look, don't go.' He ran a hand through his hair. 'I'll make you some tea—I was just going to take a break.'

In the kitchen as he filled the kettle his heart was heavy. He had spent a sleepless night thinking about Dee. She was so vulnerable at this moment, he told himself. It was always traumatic, breaking a relationship of long standing. Any older man she turned to at the moment would possibly be a stand-in for her father. Obviously she was missing having his strength and wisdom to lean on. He was determined not to allow her to fall into the age-old trap of being caught on the rebound; much as he wanted her he *wouldn't* let that happen. But how to prevent it was a problem he had no solution to. She had sensed his preoccupation just now and offered to go, so why had he urged her to stay, offered to make tea for her—prolonged the agony for himself? With an impatient sigh he raked his fingers through his hair again. Deep down he knew why. He had to make it clear to her right here and now that a relationship between them just wasn't on. If he'd been in any doubt at all about it after his sleepless night, the telephone call from Heather this morning had confirmed it. Hearing from her like that, out of the blue after months of silence, had shaken him to the core. He'd thought he'd seen the last of her, that it was simply a question of waiting for the decree absolute; but now . . . He couldn't allow Dee to become involved in anything Heather might have planned. She'd been through enough lately. He sighed deeply. He would have to be cruel to be kind, he told himself; it was the only way in the long run. But *cruel to whom?* an inner voice demanded. Sending Dee away now would be like tearing himself in half.

In the living room, Dee leaned forward from where she sat on the settee to look at some estate agents' leaflets that were strewn on the coffee table. They were mostly for small flats or town houses, little boxes like the one her father lived in, completely devoid of character. As Greig came back into the room carrying the tray she looked up.

'I've been having a look at these.' She waved the sheaf of leaflets. 'I know they're probably much more the kind of thing you're looking for, but none of them are a patch on the little Georgian house.'

He set the tray down on the table. 'Maybe not, but I've solved the problem anyway. I've managed to rent a flat from someone who's going abroad for six months. The details arrived this morning by the same post— look.' He sorted through the leaflets on the table, found what he was looking for and handed it to her. 'Here it is. It's in a block on the other side of town.'

Dee scanned the leaflet, then looked up at him with dismay. 'The rent seems awfully high. You might as well have bought the Georgian house.'

'Perhaps, but look what this has to offer. Every labour-saving mod con you can think of; no heating problems—it's all run from a central plant; no garden to toil over, and all the kitchen gadgets are built in.'

'It all sounds rather impersonal,' remarked Dee, looking at the description. 'And the rooms are terribly small, aren't they? Won't you find it claustrophobic?'

Greig bent his head over the cups. 'I shan't be in it very much and I'm not planning to do much entertaining. It's just a place to lay my head, really.'

A block of flats on the other side of town! Dee reflected that if he moved there she would hardly ever see him. She voiced the thought and he looked at her dismayed face. Resolutely ignoring the dull ache in his heart, he reached out to ruffle her hair playfully. 'That won't worry you once you get this new life of yours off the ground.'

She stared at him. Although nothing had actually been said, she had thought that *he* was to be a major part of that new life. She thought of the warmth and closeness she had known with him and the way it had blossomed into a stirring excitement that intensified each time they met. She had been almost certain that he shared the same tingling, restless desire that was, to her, so new and overwhelming. It seemed now that she had been mistaken; Greig had sensed her deepening feeling for him and was backing off. She felt her cheeks burning. She had almost made a complete fool of herself.

Swallowing her hurt and humiliation, she forced a smile. 'Claire and I had got used to having you as a neighbour. You're so well behaved and quiet, and so far you haven't thrown any wild parties.'

'Maybe your next neighbour *will* throw some—and invite you!' He leaned back, folding his arms and regarding her like an older brother. 'That's what you need, Dee,' he told her earnestly. 'To let yourself go a little and enjoy your youth now that all this trauma is over for you. Have fun!'

Inside she shrivelled. He could hardly have made it plainer: he was giving her the brush-off. 'I don't like parties much,' she told him quietly. 'At least, not that kind.' She drank the last of her tea and put the cup down on the tray. 'So you're leaving? What a pity, just when you'd settled in.' When Greig didn't reply she got to her feet. She had hoped he might ask her out this evening; ask her to help him pack—anything to be with him just for a little longer, but it was clear that he had no such intention. Perhaps he was afraid she might misconstrue his motives. Her disappointment was so overwhelming that she could feel a lump beginning to form in her throat. It thickened her speech as she said: 'Well, I've taken up enough of your time. Thanks for all the help and advice. I'll go now.'

'If I've helped, I'm glad.' Greig went with her to the door. 'It's good that things worked out better than you thought,' he said. 'Remember what I said, Dee. It's time to begin again now. Make sure and be happy this time.'

Hardening his heart, he closed the door firmly on her crestfallen face and turned to clench his fists, screwing up his face into a grimace of pain. 'Damn!' He thumped one fist into the palm of the other hand. 'Damn! Damn! *Damn!*'

CHAPTER ELEVEN

THE weeks dragged by for Dee. Bobby achieved his ambition of leaving hospital within a month of his accident, although the only way Greig would allow it was if he agreed to go to a rehabilitation centre for a short period. Here he knew Bobby would be properly supervised. He would be helped in the slow and painful business of rebuilding the muscles in his restructured limbs and would not be allowed to overdo things.

Dee heard all this through Bobby himself. Oddly, she found that they now had a much happier relationship than ever before. They could meet as friends, without all the strains and stresses they had suffered as a mismatched couple. She visited him often while he was still at the hospital and later, during off-duty hours, at the rehabilitation centre, a short bus ride from Queen Eleanor's.

Greig had left Wedgwood House for his new flat a couple of days after Dee's break with Bobby. She had hardly seen him since, and she threw herself into her work with a fervour that dismayed all those who cared about her. Standing in for absent colleagues now that the holiday season was upon them and the surgical unit found itself short-staffed, she clocked up a record number of overtime hours until Sister Fairchild began to worry about her pale face and peaked appearance. One day, about a month after Bobby's discharge from Queen Eleanor's, the Theatre Sister watched thoughtfully as Dee checked off her list of used instruments at the end of the morning list, working methodically through the routine. Concerned, she took in the pale face in which

149

the features had noticeably sharpened, and the thinness of her shoulders under the theatre gown. She shook her head. The girl was working like an automaton; going through the motions like a machine. She'd lost weight too. Breaking with that young man must have caused her more distress than she'd admitted at the time. Something was certainly still troubling her, and it couldn't be allowed to go on. She made up her mind to talk to her about it without further delay.

In the changing room as Dee stripped off her surgical gloves and untied her theatre gown Mary Fairchild looked at her. 'Are you doing anything for lunch today, Deanne?'

Dee looked round in surprise. Sister Fairchild never called her by her Christian name—not while they were on duty, anyway. 'No,' she said. 'I was just going to have the usual sandwich and a cup of black coffee.'

'Heavens, is that your normal lunch?' The older woman looked horrified. 'No wonder you look as though a puff of wind would blow you away! You really should eat properly. Come and have something with me in the canteen. I'd like to talk to you.'

Dee sighed. Now what? Claire had already been nagging her—warning her that it was only a matter of time before the eagle-eyed Sister Fairchild noticed her run-down state and took her to task. She looked up resignedly as she turned off the taps and began to dry her hands. 'All right,' she said, trying to sound enthusiastic. 'That would be very nice.'

It was too early for the rush and they found a table on the far side, close to the large windows with their panoramic views over the sprawling Midlands city. With motherly insistence Mary had recommended that Dee choose a double helping of steak and kidney pie with treacle pudding to follow.

'You need building up, my girl,' she announced,

shepherding Dee to the table she'd had her eye on, where they could talk undisturbed. She watched shrewdly as her young scrub-nurse began to eat. The girl obviously had no appetite. 'What's wrong, Deanne?' she asked, coming straight to the point. 'You're obviously fretting about something, and I can see that it's getting you down.'

Dee pushed a large, unwanted forkful of food into her mouth and chewed thoughtfully to give herself time to think. She shook her head. 'No, really—I'm fine,' she said at last.

Sister gave an impatient little snort. '*That* you're not, my girl! Even Douglas Thurman remarked on your tired eyes this morning, and you know how unobservant *he* is!' She leaned forward, her eyes and voice more gentle as she said: 'You really should be getting over your broken engagement by now. Are you still in love with that young motorcycle racer you gave up? Is that it?'

Dee looked up in surprise. 'No. Bobby and I are the best of friends. I told you, I'm fine—*really*!'

But Sister Fairchild was not so easily averted. Once she made up her mind to get to the bottom of anything she didn't rest until she had. And she felt she was no nearer getting to the bottom of this than she'd been yesterday. She leaned forward confidentially as another thought occurred to her.

'You've been doing a lot of overtime lately. You're not in any kind of financial difficulty, are you?' As Dee looked up at her with startled eyes she hurried on: 'All right, I know it isn't any of my business—except that as Theatre Sister I have a right to ask if I think something is happening which could affect my nurses' work . . .'

'I haven't any money troubles,' Dee interrupted. She laid down her knife and fork. Obviously she was going to have to offer some explanation, and it would have to sound convincing. 'Bobby's accident, and breaking our engagement, must have taken its toll of me, I suppose,' she said slowly. 'Working hard has helped, but I do feel rather tired.'

Mary wasn't entirely convinced. 'Well, as long as that's all it is . . . I haven't heard you mention any holiday arrangements. What about taking some time off?' she suggested. 'You could go and stay with your father. I don't think you've seen him for some time, have you?'

Dee shook her head. She felt her father was the last person who would want to hear about her troubles, but she wasn't going to embark on *that* subject. 'Yes, that's a good idea,' she said, grasping at anything that might bring the conversation to an end. 'I might go and spend a few days with him some time soon.'

'Next week!'

Dee looked up. 'What did you say?'

'I *said* next week,' Sister repeated firmly. 'It's an ultimatum. If you don't go along and fix it up this afternoon I shall recommend that you're suspended on health grounds. If you go on like this you'll be making a mistake in theatre, and I don't have to tell you how serious that could be.'

Dee knew when she was defeated. Her shoulders drooped and she pushed her plate aside.

Sister Fairchild relented, a little dismayed at Dee's reaction. Had she gone over the top? 'Now there's no need to look like that,' she said kindly. 'I really do think you need a break, Deanne. It's you I'm thinking of. You're a darned good scrub-nurse and I'd hate to see you running into trouble and ruining all the hard work you've put in.'

To her horror, Dee felt tears pricking the corners of her eyes. Sister Fairchild's telling off she could take; but her kind words . . . Her throat was tight as she said: 'Thanks, Sister. I expect you're right. I'll see to it this afternoon.' She looked at the plate of congealing treacle pudding and her stomach rebelled. 'If you don't mind I think I'll go now,' she said, getting to her feet.

'Oh, but you haven't finished your lunch!'

'No, I'm really not very hungry. I'll go and get that break fixed up before I do anything else.' Dee forced a smile. 'Thanks for the talk. I'm sure you're right. See you tomorrow.'

Sister Fairchild watched in dismay as Dee hurried away. The poor child had looked close to tears. She hoped she hadn't been too hard on her. She was really fond of the girl, but she'd never been much good at flowery words. Straight out with it, that was her way, always had been. She shook her head. In spite of her protests there was something badly wrong there— something the girl was bottling up, keeping to herself. Absentmindedly, she pulled Dee's plate of untouched pudding towards her. 'Ah well, waste not, want not,' she muttered to herself as she began to eat.

To Dee's surprise she found that it would be possible for her to take the following week off. She'd half hoped that the holiday rota would prevent this, but it seemed to be an unpopular week for some reason. Resignedly, she put her name down for it before going home to the flat. What on earth was she going to do with a whole week off? She wondered. The thought of staying alone in the flat with her thoughts filled her with dread—yet the idea of holidaying alone was worse!

That evening, when she told Claire about her week off, the other girl nodded with approval. 'Very sensible. You can certainly do with a break. And you'll be able to celebrate your birthday in style without having to worry about getting up early next morning!'

Claire had almost forgotten her birthday; a fact ex-pressed by the blank look on her face. Claire laughed. 'I do believe you'd forgotten that it's the day after tomorrow!' She shook her head. 'I thought as much! What *am* I going to do with you?' She shook her head in mock despair. 'Take a word of warning and make a hair appointment,' she advised. 'I'm arranging a little celebration for you myself.'

Dee sighed. 'Oh, Claire, I wish you wouldn't. I really don't feel like it.'

'I know—and that's precisely why I did it, so consider yourself out-manoeuvred!' Claire told her. 'And I'm not telling you anything else about it, so don't ask. Just make sure you look beautiful and leave the rest to me!'

Greig stood at the window of his sixth floor flat, gazing out at the view. Dee had been right about his feeling claustrophobic. The confines of the minute rooms made him feel like a battery hen and the view from the window, one of the river, its willow-fringed banks green and restful-looking, was its only salvation. Thank God he would soon be out of here!

As he gazed down at the gently rippling water far below him he reflected that even the view seemed a long way off. Everything that had made his life take on a new meaning seemed a long way off since he had left Wedgwood House—and Dee. Only his work now gave him pleasure and fulfilment, and Heather's constant attentions during the past few weeks had left him feeling as though he'd been to war.

When she had telephoned out of the blue that morning and told him that she was in the Midlands to set up a chain of modelling agencies he had had no choice but to believe her and, as far as he knew, it was the truth.

She hadn't altered, and it hadn't been long before he had seen through her cloying sweetness and her protestations that she had missed him, to the ulterior motives that lay behind her apparent change of heart. Once he saw through the devious working of her mind he had set to work to convince her that contrary to her suppositions, he wasn't about to become rich and famous on account of his two well-known patients—that his sights were no more on a Harley Street practice now than they had ever been and that, as far as she was concerned, he was as much of a dead loss as he had been during their marriage. It had taken her some time to accept the fact, and when she had, her sweetness had turned to one of the familiar impatient outbursts. She had criticised him for not making the most of his opportunities—insisting that he was missing so much of the good things of life, making it clear that she saw herself as one of these.

But Greig had long since given up trying to describe to her the rewards and the satisfaction his work gave him. He knew it was useless trying to convince her that there was more to life than cash and material benefits. He also knew that for her, his way of life wasn't even worth consideration. As she had once said herself in a moment of frustrated fury, his way was for 'saints and idiots'. And she had made no secret of which she thought he was!

Maybe she'd been right all along. Perhaps he should never have married at all, he told himself pensively as he gazed out at the evening sky. Perhaps it wasn't fair to expect any woman to share his kind of life—unless it was someone like . . . He shook his head impatiently. He had sent her away, telling himself she was too young to realise what she was letting herself in for—that by giving her up he was doing her a favour. Even now she was probably thanking him for it; picking up the threads of her life again and enjoying herself. But his eyes were dark with wistfulness as he remembered the feel of her in his arms and the deep longings she had aroused in him. When he closed his eyes he could still see her lovely face with its wide green eyes and gentle mouth. With an angry gesture he drew the curtains on the idyllic scene below. Like so much else in his life it was far beyond his reach.

Applying himself to the immediate future, he turned to dial the number of the restaurant. It was Heather's last night in town and he had promised to take her out for a farewell dinner. It was to be their final goodbye. She had at last given up on him. Now that her work here in the Midlands was over for the present she would be going back to the arms of the unsuspecting man she had left behind.

Dee wore the blue dress she had bought for Bobby's party—the one that had been destined never to take place. She had worn it only once before, on the evening Greig had taken her out to dinner, and when she slipped it on and stood before her mirror she was reminded with painful sharpness of the occasion. Looking back, she realised it had been on that evening that she had discovered that she was in love with him. Scrutinising her reflection critically, she suddenly saw the reason for Sister Fairchild's concern. There were dark smudges around her eyes and hollows under her cheekbones. She sat down at the dressing table and applied a skilful make-up, then brushed out her newly shampooed hair to curl softly over her forehead and against her neck, to hide the gaunt shadows made by her collarbone. Some of her fellow nurses had been asking her lately what diet she was on. And they made it plain that they thought she was being cagey when she told them she wasn't even trying to lose weight.

Claire had ordered a taxi to take them to the restaurant where she had booked a table, and Dee was slightly shocked when they arrived. It was one of the smartest places in town, and she knew it was outrageously expensive. She started to say so, but Claire took her firmly by the arm and hurried her inside. To her surprise there was quite a crowd waiting for them. There were two friends she and Claire had trained with, now working at different hospitals, Bill Kenlaw and a young houseman Claire had been out with several times, and last but not least, a smiling Bobby; still in his wheelchair, much to his disgust, but looking fit and cheerful, with his sister Angie and Geraldine along to make sure he behaved himself. When she and Claire made their entrance the small party applauded and sang 'Happy Birthday' slightly off-key, until Dee finally begged them to stop and sat down, blushing and laughing in spite of herself. She found herself sitting next to Bill Kenlaw, who touched her arm and leaned closer.

'You're looking beautiful this evening,' he told her, his eyes openly admiring. 'I don't quite know what it is, by you've developed an air of mystery lately—several people have remarked on it.' He smiled into her eyes. 'It's very sexy and intriguing.'

She turned to look at him, sipping the sherry the waiter had just placed before her. 'I think you're just trying to flatter me,' she told him. 'Most people call it looking washed out and run down!'

As the evening progressed Dee relaxed and began to enjoy herself, the wine and good food releasing the tension coiled inside her. It seemed to her that Bobby was the celebrity of the evening; the other members of the party all vied for his attention, wanting to hear about his recovery and his plans for the future. They had all heard about his courageous recovery. He was quite a hero and obviously much admired. But Dee didn't resent any of this. She had always hated being the centre of attention and was quite happy to stay in the background and let him enjoy the limelight. Bill was clearly delighted that she was no longer Bobby's girl-friend and seemed happy to stay in the background with her, making the most of having her to himself for once.

After the main course, at a signal from Claire, a waiter carried in a beautiful birthday cake blazing with candles, and for a few minutes, while the candles were blown out and she was encouraged to make the first cut, Dee *was* the centre of attention. 'Make a wish!' someone called; and Dee smiled. Her only wish was locked deep inside her heart, the key lost without trace.

Bobby proposed a toast and her health was drunk, then to her relief everyone settled back into informal chatter again. Bill was trying hard to pin her down to a date when he suddenly stopped talking to stare across the room. Under his breath he whistled softly.

'Pheeew!'

Dee followed his gaze. Some people had just come in and were being shown to their table by the head waiter. She couldn't see very clearly from where she was, but there was no mistaking the broad shoulders, that thick brown hair. He was wearing the smart grey suit; his 'establishment set'. Her heart lurched with the familiar excitement mingled with dismay. Greig wasn't alone. The woman with him was perhaps thirty and was drawing the attention of every man in the room. When the waiter pulled out her chair and she turned to sit down Dee caught her breath, seeing quite plainly the reason. She was beautiful, with raven black hair and large, dark-fringed violet eyes. She wore a starkly simple white dress, which contrasted dramatically with her exotic colouring. Almost without realising it Dee asked: 'Who is she?'

'His wife,' Bill told her. 'Haven't you heard? The hospital has been buzzing with it. They were supposed to be getting a divorce, but she's come back. The general consensus of opinion is that there'll be a reconciliation.' He chuckled. 'Looking at her it's hardly surprising!'

Dee's heart plummeted. No wonder Greig had been

anxious to remove himself so hastily from Wedgwood House! No wonder he wanted to remain free of possible entanglements—anything that might jeopardise his chances of getting his wife back again. Why couldn't he have confided in her? She had opened her heart to him about Bobby. She felt her cheeks burning as she turned to Bill. 'I hadn't heard, no.' Trying hard to sound unconcerned, she asked: 'How long ago did all this happen?'

He shrugged. 'I don't know exactly. It seems she got in touch again when she read about him in the papers—you know, after he did Bobby's operation . . .' He peered into her face. Her colour had faded now and she was quite startlingly pale. 'Are you all right, love?'

She was thinking how strange it was that their lives had become so closely enmeshed. Greig's wife was here indirectly because of Bobby's accident—the very thing that had brought her to the brink of the most important decision she had ever had to make. She realised that Bill was speaking to her and pushed the tangled thoughts to the back of her mind. 'What? Oh, yes, I'm fine.'

'You could have fooled me! Look, it's very hot in here; suppose we make our excuses and go on somewhere to finish up the evening?'

'I can't!' she told him. 'Claire arranged this party for me. It would be bad manners to walk out on her.'

Bill squeezed her hand. 'Go on. Claire wouldn't mind.'

Dee hesitated for only a moment. For her the evening was ruined anyway. All she wanted was to get out of the place as soon as possible, with luck before Greig saw her. The idea of coming face to face with him here filled her with heart-thumping panic. Bill was offering her the excuse she needed. She leaned across and touched Claire on the arm. 'Claire, I've had a lovely time and it was wonderful of all of you to give me a party, but . . .'

'Do I mind if you and Bill leave now?' Claire finished for her. 'Of course I don't.' Her eyes danced. 'Off you go, and have fun!'

Bill was delighted. He took her arm solicitously as they wound their way through the tables on their way out of the restaurant. Dee permitted herself one quick glance across the room towards Greig's table, but it was obscured by a bank of plants. At the door Bill stood back to allow some newcomers to pass, and suddenly the very thing she had dreaded happened—she turned and came face to face with Greig. They stared at each other, both of them equally shocked, green eyes gazed dumbly into brown, until Bill said:

'Oh, good evening, sir. I hope you're having a pleasant evening.'

'Very pleasant, thank you.' Greig dragged his gaze away from her face to smile at Bill. 'And you— something to celebrate?'

Bill threw an arm round her shoulders. 'It's Dee's birthday. A few of us got up a bit of a party for her.' Bill waved his hand. 'We were sitting over there. Bobby Carr's there too. I'm sure he'd like to say hello if you have a minute.'

Greig gave a cursory glance towards their table. 'Oh yes, so he is.' His eyes returned to hold hers again and she saw a tiny muscle in his cheek twitch and knew that he was as uneasy as she. Almost inaudibly he said: 'I'd no idea it was your birthday, Deanne. Many happy returns.'

She coloured unhappily as she whispered: 'Thank you.'

He turned to Bill. 'Surely you don't have to leave so soon?'

Bill grinned. 'Well, you know how it is. It's rather crowded there. We thought we'd rather like to go on somewhere a little more intimate and maybe dance

—sweet music and soft lights—you know the sort of thing.'

Dee winced at the fatuous remark, but when she glanced up at Greig's face he wore an expression that was impossible to read. Already he was looking towards the table on the far side of the room, no doubt anxious to get back to his wife.

'I do indeed,' he said abstractedly. 'I hope you have a happy evening. And now, if you'll excuse me . . .'

With a brief nod he was gone, leaving her feeling bleak and totally bereft. Inside she felt empty and hollow, as though someone had removed her heart and substituted an empty shell. Bill tugged at her arm.

'Come on, we'll get a taxi. I know a little place . . .'

She felt mean crying off—and even more so when, because of Bill's persistence, she had to resort to pleading a headache and sore throat before he reluctantly gave in and agreed to take her home. When they reached Wedgwood House she made it plain that she wasn't going to invite him in, and once he had gone she closed the door and gave way to the tears, scarcely knowing for whom she shed them. Poor Bill! She had treated him appallingly—simply used him to get away from the party. And poor Claire, who had laid on the party specially for her. She had let them all down—and simply because of a chance meeting with a man as remote from her as the man in the moon. She undressed and crawled into bed, curling herself into a tight ball as though to shut out the pain. Greig and his wife had looked so good together, *the perfect couple*, she told herself masochistically. *Obviously* he'd never actually stopped loving her, and now that she'd come back to him . . .

CHAPTER TWELVE

DEE's week off began badly. On Monday morning she woke to the sound of rain drumming against the window-pane. Claire had already left for the hospital, leaving her to sleep on, and the flat felt empty and cheerless.

She got up and made herself some toast and coffee, growing even more depressed as she watched the rain-drops sliding ceaselessly down the kitchen window. 'What on earth am I going to do with myself for a whole week?' she asked herself despairingly. 'I might just as well have gone in to work.'

By eleven o'clock it was clear that the rain had set in for the day, so she donned mac and headscarf and went out to the shops. She would try some new recipes and surprise Claire tonight at dinner, she decided. In the newsagents, buying an armful of magazines with which to while away the empty hours, she noticed the latest edition of her favourite nursing journal and bought a copy. She was leafing through this over coffee later back at the flat when an advertisement caught her eye: *Theatre staff wanted for newly built hospital in Saudi Arabia.* It went on to list the tempting facilities and the even more tempting salary scale. Dee fished in her handbag for a pencil and ringed the ad. Nibbling the end of the pencil, she gazed into space. That would surely be the answer—a new life. A clean break—from England and everything connected with Greig Meredith. Even if he never patched up his marriage again he had made it abundantly clear to her that he had no intention of embarking on a serious relationship with her. Staying here—seeing him every day—working with him when the occasion demanded it, wasn't going to help, and the way she felt now, it wasn't going to get any easier either. If only she hadn't let herself fall in love with him. Why hadn't she seen the danger signs? If ever there was a born bachelor Greig was it!

Making up her mind to strike while the iron was hot, she went to her bedroom and fetched a pad and envelopes, writing off for an application form there and then. This afternoon she would drop it into the post.

That evening on her return from the hospital Claire was surprised to find Chicken Chasseur on the menu, followed by an elaborate strawberry Pavlova expertly decorated with whipped cream. As Dee put the array of dishes on the table Claire shook her head. 'It all looks lovely, Dee, but you must have been slaving over it most of the day.' She looked at her friend. 'I thought you were supposed to be having a rest. You should be out enjoying yourself.'

Dee shrugged. 'You didn't happen to notice the weather on your way over, I suppose?'

'I agree there wasn't much incentive to go out today,' Claire conceded, 'but there was no need to work your fingers to the bone over a hot stove.' She looked at Dee closely. To her the other girl looked edgy and tense. 'You really should have gone away somewhere, you know,' she said gently, 'for a complete break.'

'That would have been a *bundle* of laughs, all by myself!' Dee reached for the salt. 'Believe me, I wouldn't have taken this week off at all if it hadn't been for you and Sister Fairchild nagging me into it. I'm only doing it to keep everyone quiet.'

Claire sighed. 'Dee, what *is* it that's making you so unhappy?' She laid down her knife and fork. 'Look, why don't you talk about it, love? Get it all off your chest. It was seeing Greig Meredith at the restaurant the other night that upset you, wasn't it?' She held up her hand. 'I've heard the gossip about his wife, so there's no need to explain.' She shook her head. 'I could tell you were getting—well, rather fond of him. I'm sorry, love.' She tried to coax a smile from Dee. 'Try to look at it this way: you've reached a turning point in your life. Everyone has them. It's up to you to make it a turn for the better.'

'It's not quite the way you make it sound,' Dee told her. 'It started long before the other night—just after I split with Bobby. I'd got the impression that Greig was . . .' she swallowed hard, 'well, that he felt rather more for me than just mere friendship. He was the one who urged me to break with Bobby—told me he couldn't bear to see anyone else making the same kind of mistake that he had. But when I told him my engagement was over he shied away—gave me a distinct brush-off. It was all a terrible misunderstanding. He must have been horribly embarrassed. It was a shock to find he was about to pick up his marriage again after—after all he said.'

'Had you fallen for him?' asked Claire gently. '*Really* fallen, I mean.' Dee nodded miserably and she sighed. 'Oh, Dee! You didn't tell me you felt as deeply as that. Why on earth didn't you say something? What are friends *for*, for heaven's sake?'

Dee shrugged. 'There didn't seem to be a lot of point in raking it all over. I'm trying to put it behind me, but it isn't easy here in the flat by myself every day for a week with nothing to do but think of all the things I should have done and said.' She looked up at the other girl. 'As a matter of fact I've been thinking of applying for a job abroad—look.' She passed the nursing journal across the table, opened at the ringed advertisement.

Claire read it and looked up at her friend in alarm. 'Oh—Saudi Arabia!' Perhaps it had been a bad idea to nag Dee into taking this break. She was obviously far more hurt by Greig Meredith's cavalier treatment than she'd admit if she was thinking in terms of running this far away. She decided to let the matter rest for the time being and insisted on taking Dee to the cinema after dinner. The girls spent a pleasant enough evening, each of them avoiding the subject of Greig and romantic entanglements in general. When they got home Dee assured her friend that she felt better, but as she got ready for bed in the privacy of her own room the rest of the week seemed to stretch endlessly before her like an empty desert.

She had just finished dressing the following morning when she heard a knock on the door. Opening it, she found Bill Kenlaw standing outside, a huge bunch of flowers in one hand and a box of chocolates in the other.

'Good morning.' He held out the offerings. 'I didn't buy you a birthday present last week, so I thought these might be appropriate.'

Dee took the flowers and chocolates somewhat reluctantly. 'Oh, Bill, you shouldn't. There was no need . . .'

Without waiting to be asked, he stepped past her into the flat. 'It wasn't just that. Somehow I got the impression that I'd done something to upset you the other night, so it's by way of an apology too.'

She looked up at him in surprise. 'Upset me? Of course you didn't.' She watched him close the door. It seemed he was here to stay. 'Will you have coffee?' she asked.

He grinned broadly. 'Great! Thanks.' He followed her into the kitchen and perched on a stool, watching as she arranged the flowers in the best vase she could find. 'Wonderful,' he observed. 'You've got a real knack for that.' He drank the coffee she made him and accepted a chocolate from the box when she opened it. Munching thoughtfully, he said: 'Look, don't take this the wrong way, but I heard on the grapevine that you're on holiday this week and at a bit of a loose end. As it happens I'm taking a few days' leave too. It was all fixed up months ago. I was to have been best man at a chum's wedding up in Scotland, but the whole thing's been called off so, like you, I find myself with time to kill. Don't you think it'd make sense for us to team up—keep each other company?'

Dee almost refused automatically, feeling slightly resentful. It was obvious that Claire had a hand in this somewhere. Then she took a look at Bill's hopeful boyish grin and relented. He was clearly sincere in wanting to share his free time with her, so why not? Just so long as he understood that there was nothing more than friendship on the cards. Spending time with Bill was infinitely better than being cooped up in the flat all week.

'Well, I don't see why we shouldn't,' she said slowly. She cleared her throat, searching for a diplomatic way of saying what she wanted him to understand. 'I think I should warn you, though, that . . .' Bill held up his hand.

'All right, no need. What you're trying to say is that you're not in the mood for romance, or even a little light flirtation—right?' Dee nodded, colouring a little, and he went on: 'It's all right, I understand. It's only natural, I suppose, under the circumstances. We'll just have a great time with no strings attached. I promise—okay?'

Dee smiled. 'Okay.'

Bill stood up. 'Right then. No time like the present. If you'd like to get ready we might as well start now.'

That day and the one that followed passed in a kind of blur. After a wet Monday the weather had changed dramatically and Bill took her to a large water sports centre a few miles out of town where he was a member of the aqua club. They went swimming and he tried, with moderate success, to teach her how to windsurf. He was the perfect companion for her in her present mood. He made her laugh and he was undemanding. All in all she was grateful for his company.

It was late on the second day, when they were driving home, that he said suddenly: 'Something's eating at you, Dee. What is it?'

She turned to look at him in surprise; she had thought she'd hidden her feelings quite well. 'Nothing. I'm fine.'

He shook his head. 'No, you're not—not really.' He shot her a look. 'Oh, don't get me wrong. You're trying hard enough to put a brave face on it, but I know the signs all too well. It isn't easy, is it—being thrown over for someone else?'

Dee caught her breath sharply. Surely Claire hadn't gone so far as to *tell* him about Greig?

'No,' she admitted, her eyes avoiding his. 'It hurts —but I'm not the first person in the world it's happened to and I won't be the last.' She shrugged. 'I'll get over it, given time.'

'Actually I thought it was pretty insensitive of him, turning up like that the other night—on your birthday, especially with the other woman in tow!'

She glanced at him. 'But he couldn't have known I'd be there, could he?'

Bill laughed. 'As it was *your* birthday it would have been a bit odd if you hadn't been there . . .' He broke off, glancing at her with narrowed eyes. '*Wait* a minute —are we talking about the same person?'

Too late, Dee realised that Claire had told him nothing. He had been referring to *Bobby*. 'Of course we are,' she bluffed, but already she could feel the warm, tell-tale colour staining her cheeks.

Bill pulled the car over to the side of the road and drew up. Switching off the engine, he turned to her, looking searchingly into her eyes. 'My God, don't tell me that *Meredith* is at the bottom of all this?'

'M-Meredith who?' she whispered feebly in a desperate attempt to divert him. Bill was great company, but he was notorious for his inability to keep a secret. Once he knew, it would be all over the hospital in no time. 'I—I don't know what you're talking about,' she muttered.

But it was no good; the colour that flooded her face gave her away. Bill stared at her. 'Good God, Dee, I'd no idea! You mean that you and he—that you broke off your engagement because you were . . .'

'*No!*' She shook her head vigorously. 'You're jumping to all the wrong conclusions!' She grasped his arm. 'Look, Bill, this is something very private. No one else knows. It's entirely on my side and it was a *complete* misunderstanding. Greig had nothing to do with it—nothing at *all*, and if you dare embarrass him by spreading it, I'll . . .' She broke off, suddenly conscious of the note of rising panic in her own voice. Bill grasped her hand and squeezed it.

'All *right*, love! Don't get into a state about it. I promise I won't breathe a word.' He grinned. 'Perhaps you'd better not tell me any more. After all, I can hardly tell people if I don't know the details myself, now can I?'

Dee managed to smile. He was trying to assure her that he'd keep her secret and she'd no choice now but to trust him. She swallowed hard. 'I hope you won't, Bill. Apart from anything else, if rumours started flying around it could spoil Greig's chances of patching things up with his wife, and I wouldn't want that on my conscience.'

He looked at her for a long, incredulous moment, then said quietly, 'Oh dear, oh dear. As bad as that, is it?' He shook his head. 'This explains a lot of things. No wonder you were so down the other evening! I thought you were having second thoughts about Bobby.' He winced suddenly, slapping his forehead with the palm of his hand. 'God, some of the inane things I said to

Meredith must have made you curl up! I'm sorry, love.'

Dee drew in a deep breath, feeling tears threatening again. 'Please, Bill. If you don't mind I'd rather not talk about it any more. Can we just forget the whole thing, please?'

He nodded, leaning forward to start the engine. 'Whatever you say. From now on my lips are sealed, as the saying goes.'

As they drove he glanced at her from time to time, trying to assess her mood, genuinely worried in case he'd spoiled the day for her. At last he took a chance and said: 'Dee—look, there's a party on this evening. Peter Spalding, a registrar on one of the medical firms, is getting engaged to one of the secretaries from Admin. Why don't you come with me?'

She sighed, wishing everyone would stop trying to 'take her out of herself'. 'Ever heard of the skeleton at the feast?' she asked with a wry smile.

He waved her comment aside airily. 'Rubbish! Talking of feasts, though, I've heard that the buffet is going to be something special. They're hiring professional caterers, no less!' He patted her knee. 'Go on, Dee, you're not going to condemn me to going alone, are you?' He pulled the corners of his mouth down comically. 'Imagine me standing in a corner all evening like a male wallflower, all alone with no one to dance with.'

The unlikely possibility of Bill remaining alone for more than a few minutes brought a spontaneous smile to her face and she finally gave in. 'Oh, all right then.' She looked at her watch. 'But if you're expecting me to go to a party with you, you'd better get me home as fast as you can. My hair's a mess and I'll need to wash it and have a bath before I'm fit to be seen in public!'

He glanced quickly at her tanned face and windblown hair. 'You look fit to eat to me,' he said—and meant it. Privately he thought he'd never seen her looking lovelier, but he daren't tell her so for fear of scaring her off again.

The party was to be held in the common room of the medical staff residence, and Bill had promised to call for Dee at eight o'clock. Claire was invited too, and was delighted to find that Bill had managed to persuade Dee to go. But as she put the final touches to her make-up Dee grew more and more doubtful about the evening in front of her.

'I really don't feel like a party,' she told Claire. 'I'll probably be terrible company and spoil it for Bill. I should never have let him talk me into it.'

'Nonsense!' Claire stood in the doorway, regarding her friend. She was pleased to see that the two days in the open air had lifted the jaded look that had dulled her eyes and complexion. Her eyes were brighter and the light tan she had acquired had given her a glow and a sprinkling of new freckles, which suited her. She was wearing a pale blue dress of soft cotton, teamed with white sandals, her hair brushed out loosely about her shoulders. She was looking more attractive than Claire ever remembered seeing her. 'You've got to start making a social life for yourself again, Dee,' she said. 'While you were going out with Bobby you dropped all your old friends around the hospital, and I know they missed you.' She smiled. 'There are some very nice people working at Queen Eleanor's, you know. You could do worse than cultivate some of them.'

From the twinkle in her eyes Dee knew she was talking about the male ones, and she was grateful that Bill's knock on the door at that moment saved her from replying.

By the time they reached the building known as the Med. Res. it was half-past eight and the party was getting under way. Popular taped music was playing, and from the look of the sumptuously laden buffet table on the far side of the room Bill's anticipation about the quality of the food seemed justified. The atmosphere was relaxed, with everyone in casual clothes. Bill introduced Dee to the newly engaged couple, both of whom she knew slightly, then Bill coaxed her to dance with him. An hour later, as they were gratefully sipping drinks by the open french windows, he smiled at her.

'Glad you came?'

She returned his smile. She was enjoying herself more than she had expected to. 'Yes, I'm glad I came. It's a lovely party,' she told him, smiling warmly. 'Thank you for inviting me, Bill.'

He took the glass from her hand, putting it on a table as a slow, romantic number began to play. 'Listen—I love this tune. Come and dance.' He took her hand and led her into the centre of the room where several other couples were dancing. Drawing her close, he rested his cheek against hers. As he felt her stiffen slightly he drew back his head to glance at her. 'Relax! I'm not about to start assuming anything or taking advantage.' He grinned down at her. 'You surely don't expect me to keep my distance all evening, though, do you?'

Dee smiled back at him hesitantly, feeling rather foolish. 'Of course not—it's just . . .'

'I won't have too much to drink and start getting obstreperous, if that's what you're afraid of,' he promised. 'But I can't have people thinking I've lost my touch. I do have my image to think of, you know.'

It was so typical of him that she laughed, throwing her head back to look up at him.

'That's more like it!' He squeezed her lightly, swinging her round—and it was at the moment that she caught sight of the newcomer standing in the doorway. He had obviously been watching the dancers, including her and

Bill, and the expression in his eyes wiped the smile from her face.

Greig had put on the grey suit with a crisp white shirt and a formal tie. The moment he arrived he saw that it was a mistake and he was standing in the doorway, wondering whether to go home and change. If he'd still been living round the corner at Wedgwood House it would have been simple, but now, with his flat right over on the other side of town . . . Why hadn't anyone mentioned that it was a casual affair?

Then he saw her—wearing a pale blue dress and looking heart-stoppingly lovely. She was dancing with Bill Kenlaw. He had both arms around her and she was laughing up into his face as though she hadn't a care in the world.

Trying to ignore the savage twist in his heart, he assured himself that this was *good*. It was what he wanted for her, wasn't it? Obviously she was doing just what he had advised and making a new life for herself. He'd heard she was on holiday, so he hadn't expected her to be here. Suddenly he was glad of the grey suit; it would give him a good excuse to slip away. Then she saw him, and his heart contracted as he watched the smile leave her face as their eyes met across the room. He was about to turn and slip away quietly when Peter Spalding spotted him and hurried across the room to take his arm and draw him in.

'Greig, so glad you could make it,' he said. 'Come and have a drink.' He looked round. 'Now let me see—who do you know?'

Greig heard himself muttering incoherent pleasantries as he was drawn helplessly into the throng. It seemed there was no escape. He turned—and found himself standing in the path of someone who was trying to make a dash for the door. It was Dee. For a split second their eyes met, then Peter grasped her arm.

'Ah, Dee, good! Here's someone I'm sure you know, Greig. You've probably worked with her. Dee Latimer.' He beamed at her. 'Be a love, Dee, and look after Greig, will you? Show him where he can find something to eat and a drink.'

Peter melted back into the crowd, leaving them stranded—trying not to look at each other. Dee swallowed hard. 'How are you?'

'I'm fine—and you?'

'I'm fine too.'

'I thought you were on holiday—someone said . . .'

'I was—*am*. I didn't want to go away, though. Too late to fix anything up.'

'I see.'

'Do you like your new flat?'

Greig shook his head. 'It was a mistake. I'm hoping to move again as soon as possible. I haven't even unpacked properly.'

Dee bit her lip. Of course, obviously he would be buying a house now that he and Heather were making a fresh shart. She wondered where his wife was, but couldn't steel herself to ask. Meeting like this was even more agonising than she had envisaged. She tried to smile. 'Can I get you a drink? There's some very good food over there.'

He shook his head. 'Nothing to eat, thanks. A drink would be nice. A glass of wine, perhaps.'

She raised an eyebrow at him. 'Nothing stronger?'

'No. I'm on emergency call—better not.'

Dee collected a glass of wine from the table and took it to where he was standing by the window. Greig took it from her. 'Thank you. You're not drinking yourself?' She shook her head. There was an uncomfortable silence, then he said: 'Look, don't let me take you away from your partner.'

'It's all right. He seems to be pretty well occupied at

the moment.' She nodded towards the couples dancing. Bill was now dancing with a pretty blonde girl and seemed to be enjoying himself greatly. She turned back to Greig. 'Are you—alone?' she ventured.

He nodded, sipping his wine. 'Yes. My—er—Heather went back to London last week.'

Trying not to sound bitter, she said: 'You must miss her. But then I'm sure you'll be seeing her again soon.'

He nodded. 'In all probability.'

Dee stared at him, her heart beating fast. How *could* he stand there so unconcernedly talking about the wife he was supposed to be divorcing? Suddenly she could bear it no longer. 'Why didn't you tell me?' she heard herself asking, her voice unsteady. 'Why couldn't you have been straight with me and *said* that you were picking up the threads of your marriage again? Did you think I wouldn't understand—that I'd make things awkward for you?'

His eyes widened. 'Picking up threads? What do you mean?'

But now that she had started she couldn't stop. 'I thought we were friends—at *least* friends. I let you advise me. I took your advice about my engagement. And then you just—just *dropped* me. You even moved —right to the other side of town, presumably so that you wouldn't have to see me. What kind of person do you think I am, Greig?'

Her voice had risen slightly, though there was little chance of attracting attention amid the din of music and voices. Nevertheless, Greig took her arm and gently drew her through the open windows on to the patio.

Taking her shoulders, he looked into her eyes. 'Dee, would you mind telling me what all this is about, please?'

She gulped hard at the threatening tears. 'Why did you have to come here tonight?' she whispered. 'Just when I—just when . . .'

He watched helplessly as she fought for control, the huge green eyes brimming. 'Oh, Dee,' he said despairingly, 'do you think I'd have come if I'd known you'd be here? Do you really think it isn't painful for me too? Have you never really asked yourself why I decided to stop seeing you?'

She took a deep shuddering breath. 'At first—yes. Then it became obvious that you wanted Heather back, and didn't intend anything—*anyone* to get in the way and upset your plans. If you'd only *said*, Greig, I'd have understood. But to go away like that—avoid me . . .'

'Oh, you idiot. You little *idiot!*' He shook her gently, then pulled her into his arms. 'It had nothing to do with Heather. And as for picking up the threads, as you call it, those threads were weak to begin with and they were broken long ago. Nothing's changed. My divorce is still going ahead.' He tipped up her chin to look into her eyes. 'Didn't you guess that I didn't want to catch you on the rebound from Bobby?' he asked her gently. 'He made you unhappy, and I couldn't see that *I'd* make you any happier!' he shook his head as she opened her mouth to protest. 'I was so afraid, Dee—afraid you might see me merely as a shoulder to weep on, some kind of father figure.'

She looked up at him, shaking her head incredulously. 'Father figure? Oh, Greig, you're mad! How could you think that?' She reached up to wind her arms around his neck, drawing his head down to hers, then she kissed him, putting all the desperate longing she had felt over the past weeks into her kiss. Just for a moment he seemed to resist her, then his arms closed convulsively round her, crushing her close as his mouth hungrily responded, giving her all the proof she needed that what he had just told her was true.

The kiss seemed to last for an eternity and Dee felt

suspended blissfully in time, but at last Greig released her. Drawing her head into the hollow of his shoulder, he stroked her hair, his lips moving against her forehead as he whispered: 'I've missed you so much. You're the loveliest thing that ever happened to me. But it's no good, I can't marry you—however much I might want to. It's out of the question.'

Dee stared up at him. 'Why, Greig—*why?*'

He sighed wearily. 'Oh, it's so difficult to explain to you—so . . .' There was a sudden bleeping noise and he sighed, patting his breast pocket. 'That's for me, I'm afraid. I must find a phone.' He smiled at her apologetically. 'Listen. Tomorrow is my day off. We have to talk. I'll call for you at ten and we'll go somewhere quiet—all right?'

Dee nodded dumbly, watching as he left her to walk back into the room, shouldering his way through the crowd towards the hall where the telephone was. So the rumours about him were false after all? She should be grateful for that at least. But any relief she might have felt was obliterated by the bleak echo of the words he had spoken just before he was called away: *'I can't marry you. It's out of the question.'*

CHAPTER THIRTEEN

DEE was awake at first light the following morning, her mind a mixture of hope and dread about the coming talk with Greig. Last night Claire had expressed disapproval when she heard about the proposed meeting.

'It can only make matters worse for you,' she'd said. 'Better to leave well alone.'

And Dee half agreed. If Greig had had time to tell her last night his reasons for deciding to remain a bachelor it would have been different; as it was, she had to know what it was that made him so adamant.

The lovely weather of the past two days had held. By seven it was already warm and promising to get warmer. She dressed in a lime green linen skirt and pretty top of white eyelet cotton. Watching from the window, she saw Greig's car draw up outside Wedgwood House, and was dismayed at the involuntary spiral of excitement that stirred her at the sight of the familiar figure getting out on to the pavement below. Taking herself firmly in hand, she reminded herself that this could well be the last time they met. She had better get used to regarding him as a colleague and acquaintance. That morning the post had brought her application form for the Saudi Arabian job, another reminder that her days at Queen Eleanor's were numbered. With time on her hands after Claire had left for the hospital she had filled it in, and now she picked up the long envelope from the table and slipped it thoughtfully into her handbag.

To save Greig from toiling up the stairs she picked up her jacket and let herself out of the flat, going to meet him, her heart filled of bitter-sweet anticipation.

The old ease they once knew was gone and they drove for the first ten minutes in tense silence, Greig's eyes on the road, while Dee looked unseeingly out at the passing scenery, wondering just what had happened to spoil the relaxed companionship they had shared before. Glancing at him, she asked: 'Where are we going?'

'A little place I know—off the beaten track,' he told her without returning her glance.

He looked tired, she thought. There were lines of strain around his eyes and mouth and his hands were taut on the steering wheel, the knuckles white.

The 'little place' turned out to be a thatched cottage restaurant in a tiny village two miles off the motorway, where they served coffee in the garden on fine days. Sitting at a wooden table under heavily laden lilac trees, they were sheltered from the sun that blazed down out of a hot blue sky. Dee thought ironically that it would have been the perfect setting—if only they had been here under happier circumstances.

'It's quiet in the week, but you should see it on Sunday mornings,' Greig told her conversationally as they sipped hot, strong coffee. Dee nodded, wondering whether he had brought Heather here. Somehow she still couldn't quite believe that his ex-wife wasn't at the bottom of his decision.

For a while they talked of trivial things, each of them putting off the moment of truth. And when at last he came to the point he startled her with his directness.

'Before I say anything else, Dee, I want you to know that I love you.'

Her eyes swung round to his face, but he didn't look at her, his eyes were fixed on the rose hedge on the other side of the lawn, his face expressionless, and just for one incredulous moment Dee wondered whether he had in fact spoken, or whether her mind was playing tricks.

Suddenly he turned towards her, and she caught her breath at the look in his eyes. 'It may sound odd, but it's precisely *because* of that that I'm not going to ask you to marry me.' He frowned, his heart heavy. It was even more difficult than he had thought it would be, especially when she looked at him like that. 'I'm rotten husband material, you see,' he went on. 'The worst possible. I know that from bitter experience.'

She stared at him. 'Greig, would you mind telling me just what it is you're trying to say?'

He shook his head. 'I'm too single-minded—*selfish and arrogant* are the words Heather used to describe me. And I dare say she was right.' He picked up her hand and found that in spite of the warmth of the day, it was cold. For a moment he looked down at it, lying so passive and defenceless in his own, before closing his fingers protectively round it. 'I was a dismal failure as a husband once. I don't intend to repeat that failure.' He looked at her. 'Especially with you.'

She looked up at him, able to think of only one thing to say. 'I love you, Greig,' she whispered. 'Until I met you I didn't know what love meant. We—we've always seemed so *right* together. You made me happy. What more could anyone ask for?'

He flinched as the simple words cut deeply into his heart. 'You don't know what it does to me, hearing you say that, Dee,' he told her. 'But I couldn't bear to see your love turn to hate—to see the warmth in your eyes grow cold and hard.' He paused, running a hand through his hair. 'For other doctors it's probably different. I had to work extra hard to qualify—to go without a lot of the things many people take for granted. My family went without too, to help me in the early days. I've got into the way of trying to make up for the sacrifices made for me. It's ingrained into me and I can't stop. I have to work flat out to pay back the debt, you see—it's become an integral part of my nature. I believe that a doctor who feels like that about his life has no right to ask anyone to share it.' He broke off, shaking his head frustratedly at the inadequacy of mere words to describe the compulsion deep inside that drove him. He looked at her hopefully. 'Can you understand?'

Dee shook her head slowly. 'Of course I understand how you feel about your work, and I share your feelings —up to a point. But does your life really have to be one big sacrifice?' He didn't answer, and she wanted to cry out: *Do you realise that you're sacrificing me too?* but she didn't. Biting her lip, she asked the inevitable question, the one she had been dreading: 'Are you saying that we shouldn't see each other again—at all?' Her voice was barely audible.

'It seems to be the only answer.' His hand tightened around hers as she tried to draw it away. 'Please try to understand, darling,' he said huskily. 'It's for your happiness. You deserve better, especially after Bobby.' He let go of her hand. 'You're young, Dee. You've hardly begun to live yet. There are all sorts of exciting things waiting for you out there.' Inside him there was an aching longing to tell her how much it hurt to give her up, but he hardened his heart to it.

Dee sat looking at him numbly, unable for the moment to take in the fact that he didn't want to see her again. Inside she longed desperately for the feel of his arms around her, his lips on hers; longed to reach out and make him take back the words he had just said, but her pride refused to let her. She had already made herself look foolish enough. First there had been Bobby, expecting her to take second place to his compulsive self-destruction—now Greig was virtually telling her that she could never mean as much to him as his work. Rising slowly to her feet, she walked back towards the place where they had left the car.

As Greig nosed the car out of the car park she sat staring out through the windscreen, her heart heavy. Such irony was almost unbelievable. He *couldn't* love her as he said. It was simply an elaborate way of letting her down lightly. Heather had been right: he *was* selfish, she told herself bitterly. He'd had marriage and all its demands once and he didn't want the bother of it again. Why couldn't he have been honest and said so? She remembered the envelope in her handbag and drew it out, turning to him.

'If you see a postbox will you stop, please?'

'Of course.' Greig glanced at the envelope in her hand, then back at her, questioningly. 'That looks official.'

'It's an application for a job in Saudi Arabia,' she told him, her voice cool and flat. 'I filled in the form this morning. It seems I have every reason for posting it now.' She smiled, her lips twisting bitterly. 'Maybe this holds the key to some of that excitement you were talking about just now!' A glance at his profile told her nothing. He showed neither concern nor interest, and at that moment she thought she hated him.

They came to the end of the village with its leafy tranquillity and moved on to the slip road that led to the motorway. The morning traffic had built up by now. At this time of year this stretch of motorway was used by holiday traffic heading for the coast in a steady stream —caravans, coaches and mini-buses as well as cars. Greig edged in and joined the stream and they drove in silence, each busy with their own thoughts.

It was just before the city turn-off that the accident happened. Dee heard Greig exclaim and lifted her eyes just in time to see a small car some way ahead of them spin off the road and up the bank at the side. It seemed almost to take off before rolling over, finishing up on its roof on the hard shoulder just ahead of them. Greig swerved off the road and leapt out of the car, Dee following as fast as she could.

Other cars had pulled over and stopped too, but Greig instantly took control. Grasping one man by the arm, he said: 'I'm a doctor. Will you drive to the nearest phone and call the police and an ambulance? Better ask for a fire tender too.' He began to pull off his jacket. 'Can someone please help me get the passengers out? I think we should work quickly.' Dee watched with rising anxiety as another man stepped forward and between them he and Greig began wrenching at the door on the car's offside. Running back to the car, Dee fetched the first-aid kit she remembered seeing in the glove compartment, praying all the time that the car wouldn't explode before the passengers could be removed. Back on the scene she was relieved to see Greig and his helper half carrying the driver to the grass verge. The elderly man seemed shaken but unhurt apart from bruises and an evil-looking cut on his forehead. As they lowered him on to the grass Greig turned to her, speaking quietly and urgently.

'Do what you can for him. His wife is still in the car—she looks in a bad way. The passenger side took all the impact and it looks as though her legs are badly injured.'

Dee looked fearfully towards the car. 'Please be careful!' But Greig and his helper were already on their way back. She knelt beside the man and cleaned the cut on his head as best she could, applying a temporary dressing from the first-aid kit. He was shaking violently and she slipped off her jacket and draped it round his shoulders.

'What's your name?' she asked.

'Murrell—John Murrell,' the man told her between chattering teeth. 'The wife—is she all right?'

'Try not to worry, John. They're getting her out now.'

Dee sat beside him and took his hand.

'I don't know what happened. I think it must have been a blow-out,' the man said, still dazed. 'One minute Doris and I were chatting—the next—oh, God . . .' Tears began to slide helplessly down his cheeks and his shoulders shook violently. Dee felt a stab of pity. She squeezed his hand. 'The ambulance will be here soon, and my friend is a doctor. It's lucky we were travelling behind you. Don't worry, she's in good hands.' She glanced across to where the two men were struggling to free the injured woman. A passing lorry had stopped now and the driver had provided some tools with which to prise apart the twisted metal.

The fire rescue tender, ambulance and police arrived at the same moment, and the woman was finally removed from the wrecked car and laid on the grass well away from the wrecked car, where Greig made a brief examination of her injuries. Dee asked someone to sit with the driver while she went to ask if she could help. Greig stood up and drew her aside, nodding to the waiting ambulance men.

'I'm worried about her. Both legs are broken and I suspect there might be some internal injuries too. She's still unconscious. How's her husband?'

'Shaken and terribly worried about his wife,' she told him. 'Someone is sitting with him. Can he go with her in the ambulance? I think he should be checked over too.'

Greig shook his head. 'She's in very severe shock. She may need respiratory assistance and—if she comes round—Entonox for the pain. It would upset him too much in his present state to see her like that.' He touched her arm. 'Would you mind if we took him in?'

'Of course not.'

Greig saw the woman into the ambulance and promised to follow up with her husband. Between them they helped the man into the car and Dee got into the back with him.

From his seat Greig turned to smile at the man encouragingly. 'Don't worry, Mr Murrell, your wife's in good hands and we'll have you both at the hospital in no time.'

'Is she badly hurt?' the man asked. 'If anything happens to her I don't know what I'll do.' He muttered on incoherently, and Dee took one of his cold hands in hers and began to chafe it.

'I expect you've been married a long time, John?' she said.

He turned anxious eyes on her. 'A week, that's all. We were on our honeymoon!' Seeing Dee's look of surprise, he went on: 'Thirty years we waited to get married. Doris had to look after her mother, you see. The old woman was an invalid—wouldn't let her only daughter go. She died last month at eighty-nine.' He sighed. 'If anything happens to Doris we'll have waited all that time for nothing. Life's hard sometimes.' He looked at Dee. 'People don't make that kind of sacrifice these days—and a good thing too, if you ask me. Life's too short to waste. You should take happiness when it's offered—God only knows there's little enough of it.'

Dee put her arm round the distressed man. 'She'll be all right, John. I'm sure she will.'

They drove on to the hospital forecourt and Greig pulled up at the entrance. He turned to Dee. 'See that Mr Murrell gets that cut stitched, then get him admitted. I'd like him kept in overnight for observation. I'm going to A and E to examine Mrs Murrell myself.' As they got out of the car he patted the elderly man on the shoulder. 'Don't worry about your wife. I promise you I'll do everything I possibly can.'

'Thank you, sir, I appreciate that.' John Murrell's eyes filled afresh with tears as Dee took his arm.

She watched as Greig strode away, her heart aching with love. Suddenly she was proud of his dedication, but at the same time she wondered whether he had heard the old man's words and recognised the lesson to be learned from them.

She found a porter and together they put Mr Murrell into a wheelchair and took him up to Ward E2 where he was admitted, then, promising to come and tell him the moment there was any news about his wife, Dee took the lift up to Theatre One.

Sister Fairchild was surprised to see her. 'Can't stay away from the place, eh?' she joked. Then she saw Dee's expression. 'What's the matter? Is anything wrong?'

'I wondered if you'd been alerted about an accident victim,' asked Dee. 'I was driving with Mr Meredith when we saw a bad accident on the motorway. We've just brought the victims in and I wondered . . .' She broke off as the telephone rang. Sister picked it up, replying briefly. As she replaced the receiver she looked at Dee.

'That was it, by the sound of it—a ruptured spleen and fractured tib and fib of both legs.' She began to bustle round, directing her staff in her usual brisk manner.

Dee touched her arm. 'I'd like to scrub—please?'

Sister Fairchild looked for one moment as though she were about to refuse, then she shrugged, shaking her head. 'All right. I won't pretend we can't do with you. Better change and scrub up as quickly as you can.'

When the doors of the surgeons' changing room opened Douglas Thurman came into the theatre, followed by Greig. As the patient was wheeled in and transferred to the operating table Dee looked up and caught Greig's eyes. They flashed her a quick, grateful smile.

*   *   *

The operation was a tense one. The patient was in her sixties and under trauma, but severe bleeding of the ruptured spleen necessitated an emergency operation. At one point there was fear of liver damage, and when Douglas Thurman had removed the spleen and it was clear that the liver was functioning normally Dee and the rest of the theatre staff heaved a sigh of relief. When his work was finished Greig moved in, working swiftly to repair and set the damaged legs before the patient was finally removed to the recovery room.

When her checking of instruments was complete Dee looked at Sister Fairchild. 'I promised to go and tell her husband as soon as there was any news,' she said.

Sister looked up. 'Of course. Off you go, and thanks for your help.' She called out as Dee hurried off to the changing room. 'And I don't want to see you again till next week—*whatever* happens!' Watching her hurry away, Mary Fairchild looked thoughtful. Why was the girl so involved with this particular patient—and how did she come to be travelling in Greig Meredith's car? she wondered.

It was only when Dee changed back into her outdoor clothes that she noticed that they were streaked with dirt and blood. She couldn't possibly go down to the ward dressed in them. Opening her locker, she took out the spare uniform she always kept there and slipped into that instead, bundling her soiled clothes into a paper bag. By the time she arrived on Ward E2 Greig was already there. He still wore his theatre gown, having paused only to remove his mask, cap and gloves. Dee stood at the end of the bed as he spoke gently to the elderly man.

'Your wife is going to be fine, Mr Murrell. She'll need a lot of care for a while, but she came through the operation remarkably well.'

'Thank you, Doctor. I can't thank you enough.' Tears filled the man's eyes and Dee stepped forward to take his hand. He looked up at her in surprise, taking in the uniform she wore. 'You're a nurse! You didn't tell me that. It's wonderful, isn't it—about Doris?'

Dee squeezed his hand, a lump in her own throat as she said. 'Yes, wonderful. All you have to do now is to take good care of her.'

'Oh, I'll do that all right, don't you worry.' He clutched Dee's hand tightly, two spots of bright colour flushing his cheeks. 'It's as though fate took a hand in this. If you and the doctor here hadn't been driving behind us this morning Doris might have . . .' He gulped, and Greig patted his arm.

'Don't dwell on it, Mr Murrell. Just rest now. I'll ask Sister to give you something to make you sleep, then when you wake up you can go and visit your wife.'

Dee stood up and with a final smile for the old man she left the ward quietly. She was waiting for the lift when Greig caught up with her. He touched her shoulder. 'Thank you for helping, Dee,' he said quietly.

She turned to look at him. 'It's my job too, remember.'

'But you're off duty.'

'So are you!' She shook her head at him as anger suddenly surged up in her like a volcano. 'Dedication isn't your own personal prerogative, you know!' she flung at him. 'It's just that some of us are capable of other emotions too—to our cost!'

She turned and walked quickly away from him, ignoring him when he called after her. Anger still driving her, she ran down all four flights of stairs and most of the way back to Wedgwood House. Inside the front door she paused to catch her breath before climbing the stairs to the flat. By the time she reached the top landing her heart was hammering, half with exertion and half from the anger-induced adrenalin pumping through her veins. Going through to the kitchen, she pulled out the ancient washing machine and began to fill it, emptying the paper bag full of soiled clothes into it and throwing in soap powder. The action seemed to symbolise her feelings. She had dressed so carefully this morning, little knowing that her clothes as well as her heart would finish up crumpled and torn. In a defiant gesture she dashed away the angry tears that trickled down her cheeks. Never again would she allow herself to fall in love, she promised herself aloud—especially not to a dedicated man. In future *she* would be selfish—*she* would call the shots. There would be no more heartache. Not for her— Deanne Latimer!

She failed to hear the front door open and close above the noise of the washing machine, and Greig stood in the doorway for several minutes watching as she applied herself furiously to her task. As she worked she muttered angrily to herself, and the fevered vows she made came to him in snatches as he stood there: *never fall in love again—dedicated man—no more heartache.* Then she turned suddenly and gasped with shock as she saw him standing there. His heart twisted as he saw the tears glistening in her eyes. He reached out a hand to her, but she stepped back.

'Go away!' she told him tearfully.

'Dee, I . . .'

'I *said* go away! Haven't you done enough? You've told me there's no room in your life for me and I've promised to go away. What more do you want me to do?'

'Marry me.'

'Isn't Saudi Arabia far enough for you?' she rushed on heedlessly. 'If I could sign on for the next moon-shot I would!'

'*Shut up, girl!*' Greig took a step towards her and grasped her by the shoulders, his eyes dark. When he spoke his Welsh accent was very much in evidence. 'Be quiet, you little idiot, and *listen* to me! You heard what that old man said this morning. He made me feel humble—made me see what a fool I was letting you go when you're all I've ever wanted for myself. Working together—fighting for a future for those two people opened my eyes, made me see the stupidity of giving up the things we want when life is so short and tenuous.' His eyes searched hers as he drew her closer. 'I want *you*, Dee. I've wanted you right from the first day I saw you—I couldn't make myself stop wanting you, even when I thought you belonged to someone else—even when I told myself I'd only make you miserable. And now I've made my mind up. Whatever other sacrifices I make, I can't let you go.'

Dee swallowed hard, feeling as though all the breath had been knocked out of her. He'd put her through hell these last few weeks and she hadn't quite forgiven him. 'Sup—suppose I don't want *you* any more?' she challenged. 'Suppose I don't want a dedicated surgeon for a husband? Suppose you've talked me out of it?'

The silence that followed seemed endless. Greig looked down at her, a hint of uncertainty in his eyes. Her mouth felt dry and her heart slowed almost to a stop as he asked quietly: 'Have I? *Have* I, Dee?'

She took a deep trembling breath. When he looked at her like that she almost melted with love for him. When she spoke her voice was hardly more than a whisper: 'You—might have.'

The determined look she knew so well glinted in his eyes as he said: 'Then I'll just have to bloody well talk you *into* it again, won't I?' Before she had time to reply his lips were on hers, his arms crushing her close. Any thoughts she had had about holding him at arms' length, punishing him for the unhappiness of the past weeks, dissolved as his kiss claimed her, body, mind and soul, turning her knees to water and shattering all the resentment she had felt.

When he raised his head briefly to ask: 'Well, *will* you marry me, Dee?' she had difficulty in finding a voice with which to say 'Yes.'

He threw back his head and gave a sudden laugh of relief. 'Thank God! Back there at the hospital I thought —I was afraid I might have ruined everything.' He hugged her hard. 'Tell me *when*. Now, this minute. I'm not letting you go till you do.'

Dee shook her head, a laugh bubbling up inside her as she suddenly realised what he was wearing. 'Greig Meredith! Who else but you would propose in theatre greens?' she demanded. 'Do you have any idea how you must have looked, tearing after me like that?'

Greig looked down at himself, then joined in. 'Maybe people around here had better get used to it,' he said, pulling her close again. 'Because from now on I intend to stay close to you—in theatre greens or anything else.'

As she hid her face against his shoulder Dee smiled. It was all she had wanted to hear.

 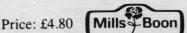

Mills & Boon

YOU'RE INVITED TO ACCEPT
4 DOCTOR NURSE
ROMANCES
AND A TOTE BAG

 FREE!

Doctor Nurse

Acceptance card

| NO STAMP NEEDED | Post to: Reader Service, FREEPOST, P.O. Box 236, Croydon, Surrey. CR9 9EL |

Please note readers in Southern Africa write to:
Independant Book Services P.T.Y., Postbag X3010, Randburg 2125, S. Africa

YES! Please send me 4 free Doctor Nurse Romances and my free tote bag – and reserve a Reader Service Subscription for me. If I decide to subscribe I shall receive 6 new Doctor Nurse Romances every other month as soon as they come off the presses for £6.60 together with a FREE newsletter including information on top authors and special offers, exclusively for Reader Service subscribers. There are no postage and packing charges, and I understand I may cancel or suspend my subscription at any time. If I decide not to subscribe I shall write to you within 10 days. Even if I decide not to subscribe the 4 free novels and the tote bag are mine to keep forever. I am over 18 years of age   EP23D

NAME _____

(CAPITALS PLEASE)

ADDRESS _____

_____

_____

_____ POSTCODE _____

The right is reserved to refuse application and change the terms of this offer. You may be mailed with other offers.as a result of this application. Offer expires September 30th 1987 and is limited to one per household.
Offer applies in UK and Eire only. Overseas send for details.